I0690611

OF LEATHER AND VANILLA

First Edition

Published by the Nazca Plains Corporation
Las Vegas, Nevada
2014

ISBN: 978-1-61098-379-2
E-Book: 978-1-61098-380-8

Published by
The Nazca Plains Corporation®
4640 Paradise Rd, Suite 141
Las Vegas, NV 89109-8000

PUBLISHER'S NOTE

Of Leather and Vanilla is a work of fiction created wholly by Richard Andrews' imagination. All characters are fictional and any resemblance to any persons living or deceased is purely by accident. No portion of this book reflects any real person or events.

Cover Photo, Fleshblack
Art Director, Blake Stephens

I would like to dedicate the stories of this book to all of my close friends in the leather and gay community in the San Francisco Bay area. My life has been greatly enriched by their friendship.

OF LEATHER AND VANILLA

First Edition

Richard Andrews

CONTENTS

CHAPTER ONE

SUBSTITUTE DAD

The sun was starting to set, as I wandered down Telegraph Avenue, from the University of California campus. The wind was blowing gently and there was a slight chill in the air. I had just finished the last final test of my senior year at Cal Berkeley. The street was almost empty, as many of the stores along the avenue were beginning to close. This moment was a quiet and perfect ending to the hell that I had just gone through with taking a final exam in the hardest class that I had this year.

I could not help thinking, that whoever invented final exams, must have been some sort of strange academic masochist. My brain feels like it's been fried.

I was looking forward to a few beers and a nice quiet evening at home, when I heard a familiar voice yell, "Hey, Jim!" I looked across the street to see Mike, an old friend of mine from New York City.

As I waved back, I could see that he had a young blond man with him. After getting my attention, he walked across the street, slapped me on the back and said, "Hey Jim, I been trying to get hold of you. Don't you ever answer your phone?"

"No, not lately, I've been studying for and taking my finals."

Mike's young companion was now standing behind him, looking me over, like he was taking inventory. He seemed especially interested in the big bulge in my jeans. My gaydar went off. This dude was gay and real horny. I smiled politely at him, he smiled back.

"Jim, I would like to introduce you to the young man that I have been tutoring for the last year. "Jim, this is Scott." I shook his hand, as he stepped forward and grabbed my crotch with his other hand. "Nice piece, dude." I shoved him back really hard, almost knocking him on the ground. "What's the fuck is wrong with you!"

"I was just trying to get to know you better. What's your problem?"

I gave him a hard look and said, "Look, I didn't give you permission to get friendly with me." He looked at me like he was offended. "Well, you really think you're hot shit, don't you!"

"No, but I am thinking about kicking you butt down to the next corner!" The young man suddenly, acted as if he were scared. He threw up his hands and said, "I'm sorry, I'm really sorry." He then backed away and sat on a nearby parked car, silent, with his head down.

It was strange, but Mike actually looked a little amused, about how I had just put his young friend in his place. He put his hand on my shoulder and said, "Can I talk to you in private for a minute?"

After walking down the block about twenty feet, Mike turned and looked at me with a more serious look on his face. "Sorry Jim, my friend Scott is still a little shy of basic social skills." As for why I have been trying to get hold of you it's because I want to talk to you about taking a job that will soon be open, that pays really good money and I know that you can handle it." All of which, was a little confusing to me. But, Mike knows me and I agreed to talk to him the next day, after I get finished lifting weights and swimming some laps in the outdoor pool, at the Cal Rec Center.

As Mike and his ill-mannered friend left, his friend turned his head to take one final look at me. He smiled. Well, it looks like I didn't hurt his feelings much. That is one horny young man. But, I will give him his due, he has nice looking ass.

The next morning, as I was taking a shower at the Cal Rec Center, before going outside to the pool, to swim some laps, I started to think about how much attention I usually get, when I walk around the outside of the pool. Since, I am 6'2" tall, with 230 pounds of well-defined muscle on my frame, not to mention the big bulge in my small swim trunks, I usually attract a good deal of attention.

After a heavy finals schedule and a good night's sleep, I am in the mood to show it off. Who knows, I just might meet someone special today. I could sure use a special person in my life.

Outside, on one side of the pool, the bleachers were more than half-full. I quickly noticed, several young men, giving me the once over. It felt good. Then I suddenly noticed that the guy that was with Mike yesterday was in the bleachers checking me out. He saw me staring at him. He smiled. Well, it looks like he definitely approves of how I look. Shit! I'm out fishing for a hot, young stud and I get eyed by a horny, blond, pretty boy.

The young man stayed in the stands, while I swam my laps. He never took his eyes off of me. As I finished my laps and headed for the showers, I could feel his eyes, checking out my well-developed ass.

My meeting with Mike was scheduled for 11:00A.M., in front of the Student Union Building.

Mike was waiting for me when I arrived. He seemed eager to tell me about this new job that he wants me to sign up for.

"You know Jim, this last year I've had a real dream job for a student. The pay is great and I really don't have to work very hard." My ears started to perk-up. Oh shit! This job has something to do with that fouled mouthed young dude that was with Mike yesterday.

I looked at Mike and said, "Don't tell me, it involves babysitting that over sexed, blond, pretty boy, doesn't it." He just nodded in agreement. I groaned, "Oh man, you know I'm not the baby sitting type, why do you think that I would be interested in a job like that?"

"Because Jim, I know you, you and I were hustlers together, in New York City, for two years. I know what you can handle and I know that you can use a lot of fresh cash right now. Plus, I owe you, for the time you kept those two hoods from cutting me up."

"You don't owe me anything. Yes, I am low on money right now. But, I can get a summer job to tide me over and in the fall my scholarship money will pay the expenses for grad school. I'll survive.

Mike just stared at me and smiled. "Can you get a summer job that will pay you $2,000 per week, plus bonuses?" He now had my full attention. "You're telling me, that you get $2,000 a week, for just tutoring that young man. Give me a break Mike, no one's going to pay you that type of money for tutoring their son."

"You're right, I'm not just a tutor; I am more like a substitute dad."

"What are your duties, with this so called job?"

"Well, it is simple, I help him with his homework, try to develop some good qualities in him, keep him off the streets and away from bad influences."

"How do you keep him off the streets and away from the usual jerks?"

"Well, I keep him from getting to horny."

"Well, you weren't doing a very good job of it yesterday, Mike. The dude was all over me." Mike just nodded his head and smiled. "That was because Scott thinks you are really hot."

The idea of making $2,000 a week, of badly needed cash, kept my attention as Mike explained the details of the job.

Mike told me, that one year ago, the young man's father found out that he was not adjusting well, to his first year at Cal Berkeley. He was starting to go off the deep end. He was hanging out with street trash on Telegraph Avenue, smoking weed and hiring hustlers from ads in gay newspapers. His favorite hustler was, yes you can guess, my old friend Mike.

Since, the father is a very rich man, a single parent, who is seldom home, he decided to hire Mike, as substitute dad. The effort paid off, the kid settled down and became a very disciplined student.

Since, Mike is going to graduate from Cal and go back East, he wants to find someone to take over his job. Someone, he knows can handle Scott. Naturally, my name came to mind.

"You mean Mike, that, I would be expected to be this rich young pricks sex toy and have to please him by sucking his dick and letting him fuck me any time he wants?"

"No Jim, you have it backwards. He is an eager bottom. He will suck your dick and you will fuck him. Anything else is up to you. By the way, Scott is a fantastic fuck, one of the best that I've ever had."

The more Mike described this so called substitute dad job, the more attractive it looked. Hell, I could always buy some duct tape for his mouth problem. So, in the end I told Mike that I would interview for the job. He said that he would talk to Scott's father and have him phone me to arrange an interview date.

That night the phone rang, it was Scott's father Mr. Burns. We had a nice long conversation, about his son and the duties of the job. Because Mike was in good standing with Mr. Burns and he recommended me, getting an interview was easy.

While getting dressed for my interview with Mr. Burns and Scott, I went over what Mike had told me. "Remember, Mr. Burns will be no problem. But, when you first talk to Scott, he may try to run a, rich little asshole game on you. Don't let him get away with it and you won't have any real trouble with him.

Looking over my clothes, I couldn't help but laugh a little, at the idea of trying to figure out what I should wear to an interview with a rich little asshole. In the end, I decided to dress well. I picked out a nice sport coat and tie, with matching slacks and shoes.

I figured that showing up for an interview, in a mansion house, with a corporate CEO, wearing my usual jeans, tennis shoes and tea shirt, would set the wrong tone.

The address, Mr. Burns gave me, was about seven blocks from my apartment, up in the Berkeley Hills. Since, it was a sunny day I decide to walk.

The house was a large refurbished brownstone mansion in a high-class section. I walked up the stairs and pushed the doorbell. As I waited, I adjusted my tie and combed my hair. The door opened, I smiled, as I extended my hand to greet Mr. Burns. After being introduced, Mr. Burns invited me into the entry hall of the house. In the background I could see Scott, dressed in a dark colored, Armani suit. I half smiled, as I started to think, he's going to pull a rich bastard act on me, just as Mike said. It's good that I decided to dress well. Wearing a coat and tie will help to cancel out his piss elegant suit.

I felt Mr. Burn's hand grip and squeeze my left shoulder, as he said, "Good to see that you decided to come, my son is looking forward to meeting you."

"Oh, we've already meant."

"Really, I didn't know that."

"Yes, Mike introduced me to your son on Telegraph Avenue, last Friday." I looked at Scott, with a stern look, he looked a little startled and quickly looked down at the floor. I smiled a little, as I turned to talk to Mr. Burns, so far, so good.

At this point, Scott left and started to walk up the stairs to the second floor and left his father and me alone. "Well Mr. Burns how will this interview be handled?"

"My son and I just got back from church and I have to leave shortly for a business meeting, so it will be up to you to figure out how you want to handle the interview with my son. I will be back in about 5 hours, so you will have sufficient time to get to know Scott and decide if you want the job."

I have to leave now; Scott is in his room upstairs, second door to the left." Mr. Burns than shook my hand and said, "Good luck, son."

After Mr. Burns left, I was left standing in the living room, mentally going over my next move, in what could turn out to be a real mind fuck trip. Hopefully, in the end, it will be Scott's mind that gets fucked.

When I got to Scott's room, the door was already open and I walked in. Scott was seated in a high back leather chair, near the bedroom window. The morning light, shined on his face and blond hair, accenting the fact that Scott was a very pretty young man.

Looking at Scott, seating in that chair, in a suit, with the tie undone, reminded me of that character Justin, on the T.V. series, Queer As Folk. Well Scott, get ready to meet the Navy Seals trained, leather version of Brian.

Scott quickly noticed me in his bedroom doorway. He looked at me with hateful glare in his eyes. "So, Mr. Muscle head, if you think that you can tell me what to do, think again, no one is going to run my life!"

I gave him a cold stare; he looked down at the floor, a good sign. His attitude said, no way, but I could see a bulge developing in his pants. Scott's half-hard dick, told me that I could win this match. I walked over to his chair, leaned over and put my hands on the armrests, with my face only inches from Scott's. "Look boy! If you want to talk to me, you will call me Sir or Mr. Cole and when I work with someone, I'm in charge. You got that little boy!" Scott looked startled; he squirmed in the chair, as I stood up. I could see that his cock was now hard and throbbing. Scott was really getting turned-on by this scene. His cock was turning out to be a great lie detector.

"Well, Well –, what will you do with me, if I decide to let you run my life. I was starting to make progress. "I will change you into a well-manned, educated, well-built young man. Someone that your father and I can be proud of."

"What makes you think that I want any of that shit, Mr. Dictator?" I looked at his crotch. His cock was about to pop out of the top of his pants. "Because Scott, of the rewards that I will give you for being a good boy."

"What could a guy like you offer me that I would possibly want?" After listening to this jerk-off rich boy, run his mouth and seeing that his cock was saying that he was lying, I decided to call his bluff.

I walked over to the right side of the armchair, unzipped my pants, exposing a thick, half-hard, nine-inch cock. Scott just stared at my cock and didn't say a thing. I than grabbed the back of his head and pushed his face on to my cock. I rubbed his face with my cock several times and when he tried to lick my cock, I pulled his head back. Scott just sat silently, wide-eyed and said nothing, as I put my cock back into my pants. "Now Scott, if you are a good boy, you will get my big man cock, in your mouth and up your ass as a reward."

With that, I walked over to the door, turned to look at the still silent boy in the armchair and said, "Also, if you are a really good boy, I will let you spend the night with me. Well, if we have a deal, have your father phone me." With that, I walked down the stairs and out of the front door.

On the walk home, I went over what had happened. Wow! That was a real trip. The expression on Scott's face, after I rubbed it in my crotch, was worth the effort. But, one thing was a little puzzling, why did he smile, from ear to ear, when I mentioned letting him spend the night with me? I thought he was a hard-core cock hound and not a relationship-minded person.

When I finally, got home to my apartment, about dinnertime, the phone was already ringing. It was Mr. Burns. "Hello, Mr. Cole."

"Yes, I just got in."

"Well, I don't know how you did it, but you really impressed my son. As a matter of fact, he begged me to hire you as his tutor."

"Well, it's good to hear that we hit if off (it's hard to figure this boy)."

"So, if you want the job, it's yours." I had to thing for a moment. Hell, I can handle this scene. "Yes, Mr. Burns, I'll take the job. I think that I can really help your son develop into someone you can be proud of."

"O.K. then, your first day with Scott will be this Monday. Is that alright with you?"

"Yes, no problem."

"Then be at my house at 3:30 P.M. Scott will let you in; I will be out of town for several days. Good luck with Scott. He needs a person like you in his life." After I hung up the phone, I smiled. Well, I can sure use the extra $2,000 a week and this is not the first job I've gotten because of my buffed bode and big dick.

When I arrived at the Burns mansion on Monday, I fully expected Scott to pull another little rich asshole game on me. But, I was pleasantly surprised, when Scott answered the door and politely asked me to come in.

In a rather humble voice, he said that he was very sorry for acting like a jerk during our interview and that he wanted me to be his new tutor. Also, he confirmed that we had a deal and I was in charge.

I took Scott into the living room and we both sat on the couch. I wanted to discuss what we would be doing that day and the rest of the week. Scott really smiled, when I told him he would be going to the gym with me and that I was going to put a lot of muscle on his body. Scott wanted to weight train, but Mike did not go to the gym.

After seeing how Scott reacted to the idea of being my gym-training partner, I decided to get started on getting him into the weight-training routine that day. But, first thing first, I needed to know certain things.

"Well Scott, do you have any gym clothes to wear today."

"Yes sir, I have several sets of gym stuff in my room."

"Well, run up and get your gym outfit ready and while you're up in your room, strip down, I need to see what I have to work with."

"Scott smiled and said, "Yes, Sir."

He then, quickly got up and almost ran up the steps to his room. I smiled a bit. The boy was eager.

Ten minutes later, when I walked into Scott's room, I expected to find him wearing only his underpants. But, instead he was totally naked, with a half-hard cock. The definition of strip down seems to have more than one meaning.

I told Scott to stand in front of the big mirror that was on the closet door. "Now Scott, stand still, I am going to inspect every inch of you. It will help me to design your training routine. At this point, I started to walk around him, visually inspecting his naked body. Scott was about 5'10" tall and I would say about 155 pounds. He had very little body hair and beautiful smooth, healthy looking skin and about an 8" now throbbing hard cock. But, what really caught my eye was his fantastic looking hairless, bubble butt. Physically, Scott is what is called, a chicken hawk's wet dream. Scott's father had made a good decision, when he hired Mike to keep this high quality piece of chicken off the streets.

I now started to physically inspect Scott. As I probed and grabbed almost every muscle in his body, he never said a word and he showed lots of signs, that he really enjoyed the rough feel of a man's hands on his naked body.

This new bit of information caused me to rethink how I was going to handle Scott. Contrary, to my first impressions about Scott, this boy actually craved to be touched or man handled by a man.

After I finished with my inspection, I told Scott to get dressed. He seemed a little disappointed. I know that he wanted my cock, but he has not earned it yet. After he got dressed, I went over my findings with him. I told him that he had very good posture, a good frame and the right amount of muscle tissue, if he wanted to really start to build up his body. He seemed pleased and very eager to get started. So we packed up his gym stuff, picked up mine at my apartment and headed to the gym.

While Scott had changed a lot in the first couple of weeks of our relationship, a fact that made me very suspicious, I'm not saying that I didn't have any problems with him. He would on occasions, have a temporary relapse, of his mouth problem. So, whenever he ran off at the mouth, I would give him a cold stare or slap the back of his head. He would than correct his language. The boy was trying hard to learn new ways. This was encouraging.

On the day that Scott was to get his first reward day, I picked him up at his home, we were going shopping. The whole day Scott was a perfect gentleman, he was in good humor and he smiled almost all the time. Scott knew that he had been a good boy and he was going to get laid.

After we finished dinner, at a small restaurant, on Telegraph Avenue, we started to walk back to my apartment. Scott smiled all the way to my apartment. Every once in a while, I would look down at the growing bulge in his pants. By the time we entered my apartment house, Scott's dick was rock hard. This boy was overheating fast. God was he horny.

After we entered my apartment, I shut the door and then turned to face a smiling Scott, standing silently with his hands behind his back. I looked at him and smiled. "Well Scott, how do you think you did these last few weeks? Do you believe that you were a good boy?"

"Yes sir, except for a few mouth problems. I will do better in the future. But, what is important is what you think Mr. Cole."

"Well Scott, I can say that we started off in a bad way, but that you have started to redeem yourself, I'm impressed with you so far." This statement caused Scott to smile and say, "Thank you, Sir."

Scott you have earned a reward for making a lot of progress. I'm going to go into the bedroom for a few minutes. When I return, I want to see you naked and ready to learn a few lessons about how to please a man."

"Yes, Mr. Cole."

As I walked into the bedroom, I could hear the sounds of shoes hitting the floor, a belt buckle being undone and zipper being opened.

When I returned to the living room, wearing just my gym trucks. I found Scott naked, with an unexpected new twist. He was on his knees, with his hands behind his back and his head nearly touching the floor. This boy was kinkier than I thought. But, kinky or not, I knew how to play his game.

I walked over to where Scott knelt on the floor and put my bare feet on both sides of his head. Without even being asked, he started to lick and kiss my bare feet and ankles, as I started to message his naked back with my hands. He moaned and, "Yes Daddy, play with me."

When he finished licking my feet, he started up left leg, to lick around my kneecap, as I ran my hands down his back and slapped his bare ass again. I wanted to see how he would react. He moaned and said, "Spank me daddy, and spank me good."

Before I walked back into my living room, I had expected to run Scott through a very basic suck and fuck session. But, he was far more experienced than I expected. This scene was starting to really turn me on. As Scott began to rub the back of his head between my legs, my cock felt like it was going to bust out of my gym trucks, so I backed away from Scott and dropped my shorts.

My cock stood at attention, only inches from Scott's face. The boy sat silently on his knees, staring wide-eyed at my now throbbing cock. He slowly licked his lips.

He wanted my cock, he wanted it bad. I grabbed the back of his head and shoved his face in my balls. "O.K. Boy, lick my balls." I moaned a little and my body started to shake as I felt his hot wet tongue lick my balls from one side to the other.

My little rich boy was just as turned on as I was. His cock was pulsating up and down, like a horny dog, that was about to mate.

As he licked my balls, Scott's eyes were fixed on my wildly throbbing cock, as it bounced against the sides of his face and his forehead. As his eyes started to beg for a chance at my cock, I told him, "Suck my dick, boy!" Scott eagerly started to lick my shaft from my balls all the way back up to the head. He rolled his tongue around the tip a few times and then he went down on my cock in one quick motion.

The sensation of his hot moist mouth and his tongue messaging my cock shaft, almost down to my hair, took me by surprise. I had not expected this pretty little rich kid to be such an expert cocksucker. I loved the feeling. I can't remember when I had felt such a pleasurable sensation. The boy was good and really liked his work.

After about 20 minutes, my cock got hard as a rock and my body started to tense up. As I let out a loud moan, I grabbed the back of Scott's head and shoved my cock down his throat.

My cock stiffened one more time, as I started to pump, stream after stream, of hot cum down Scott's thirsty throat. The boy eagerly swallowed all of it.

After my body relaxed, I looked down at Scott, knelling at my feet, cum dripping from one side of his mouth and smiled. "Good work boy!" Scott smiled, and said, "Thank you sir, it was my pleasure."

As Scott sat, naked at my feet, I could see that his cock was aching for relief. This boy deserved another reward. I leaned over, put my hands under his armpits and lifted him up on his feet. His throbbing cock, just bounced up and down.

"Well Boy, you did real well, so I am going to give you another reward. I'm going to show you how to please and satisfy a man, from the head down."

I moved closer to Scott, put one finger on his moist lips and said, "We will start with a little lesson on making out." Scott smiled, as I took my hand and raised his chin and started to kiss his hot wet lips. He moaned a little, as I started to probe his mouth with my tongue, as his cock started to rub against my still hard dick.

As Scott, became more and more turned on, I started to kiss the sides of his face, nibble lightly on his chin and ear lobes, as I ran my hands down his back, until I was lightly messaging the crack of his ass. His body started to squirm, as I moved down his torso, kissing and licking, until I was playing with his left nipple with my tongue. After a few minutes of licking and lightly biting his nipple, I lifted up his left arm and started to lick all the way around his almost hairless armpit, as my other hand lightly messaged his left side of his torso. Scott began to shake and squirm, as he said, "Oh God, Oh God."

As I moved over to lick and lightly bite his right nipple, I started to message his still wet left nipple, with my fingers. He moaned. As I finished playing with his right nipple, Scott automatically lifted his arm up and let me lick his right armpit, as I messaged his side. His body shock. "Oh God, that feels sooo good.

After finishing with his armpits, I slowly kissed my way down his chest, until my hot, wet tongue, was messaging his balls, as my hand pumped his cock. As Scott's moans started to get louder and louder, like he was close to cumming, I pinched the head of his cock and blew cold air on his wet balls. I don't want this supper horny boy to cum just yet.

When Scott showed signs that he was relaxing, I started to lick my way up his shaft and my tongue began to play with his wildly pulsating cock, as it bounced up and down, with each lick of my tongue, just before I took his whole cock into my mouth, right down to the hair.

Scott let a loud moan and his body shook, as I repeatedly swallowed the full length of his cock, as I lightly messaged the sides of his kneecaps and the back of his knees.

When I had worked my way down his legs and started to message the sides of his feet, his cock suddenly got rigid and his body began to really tense up, as he moaned loudly, "Oh God, I'm going to cum!"

I grabbed his ass checks and pushed his stiff cock down my throat, just as he let out a loud moan and started to shot a big loud of hot sweet cum down my throat.

As Scott's cock started to relax, I slowly licked my way up his chest, until I could grab the back of his head and pull it back, as I gave him a long, deep kiss, as my hand continued to slowly stroke his cock. Scott continued to moan and mildly shake as I pumped the last drops of cum out of his still throbbing hard cock.

When he was completely spent, I put both of my hands on his shoulders and put his head on my shoulder, as I lightly messaged his back, clean down to the crack of his ass. He contently moaned and put his arms around me. I than started to use my fingers to probe soft pressure points in his back. This technique caused him to moan loudly and repeatedly say "Oh god, Oh god that feels soooo good.

As I continued my back message, I whispered in his ear, "Well boy, did you learn anything tonight. His head rose up and he smiled, "Yes Sir, I learned a lot and I hope that you will teach me a lot more."

With such an eager pupil, how could I refuse such an opportunity? I grabbed Scott by the hair on the back of his head and led him over to my couch. I than slapped him on his bare ass and told him to lie down on his stomach with a cushion under his hips. He smiled and eagerly followed my orders. This eager bottom knew he was about to get fucked.

After putting some Lube on my throbbing hard cock, I spread his ass checks and slowly drove my big cock into his ass. His body started to tremble as I began to thrust my cock deeper and deeper into his willing ass. In only a matter of minutes Scott was loudly moaning and his body shook like he was really enjoyed being fucked long and hard. Mike was right this boy loved to be fucked.

For the next hour, I fucked him in several different positions, each time driving him almost to the level of cumming, before I would back off. Finally, while I had him on his back, sweat dripping from our bodies, I shot my load at the same time as he did.

Satisfied I withdrew my cock and lifted Scott off the couch, stood him up and gave him a long, deep kiss. Suddenly he said, "Did I please you Sir?" I just smiled and nodded.

After taking a shower, we watched a few hours of T.V., with me sitting on the couch, wearing my gym shorts and Scott sitting naked at my feet. When I was ready for bed, I ran my hands down his chest and grabbed his balls. He looked into my eyes, as I asked him, "Well boy, do you want to spend the night." He smiled, ear to ear, "Yes Sir, very much."

When we both stood up, I gave Scott a big kiss. "That's for being a good boy tonight." I than grabbed him by his now hard cock and led him to my bed.

Early the next morning, as a cool breeze, from an open window, made our skin tingle, I pulled back the covers on my bed, lubed up my cock and I started to royally fucked Scott again, for almost an hour. Scott loved it. He got so turned on that he came without even touching himself. It was a great way to wake up.

The boy seemed so pleased, that he volunteered to clean up my apartment and to fix a meal, while I finished some work on my computer.

I'm beginning to figure out who the real Scott is. He is not the loud mouth, rich kid, with a bad attitude, that I at first intensely disliked. Mike only figured out half the truth. He thought that Scott was just and eager bottom, with a mouth and attitude problem.

But Mike is an accounting student, he has no leather experience and he is not good at reading people.

The fact is Scott is a submissive personality, who only needed to meet the right dominate male, who could handle him. The way he has been reacting to me, indicates that I have what he wants.

After finishing my computer job, I got a cup of coffee and sat down on the couch. As I sipped my coffee, I watched Scott eagerly clean my apartment in the nude. I started to think, that I have the whole summer to really train Scott, both in body and mind, before we both have to hit the books again in the fall. I kept picturing in my mind, what Scott will look like, with 30 pounds of well-defined muscle on his frame and how much progress I can make with him in the next two years.

As I finished my coffee, I started to think. You know, I am one lucky guy. To think, I am going to be paid $100,000 a year, for the next two years, to basically train my own daddy's boy. Man it doesn't get any better than this. I smiled, put my hands behind my head and quietly said, "Thank you Mike, I owe you one."

CHAPTER TWO

SLAVE INTERVIEW

It had been fifteen years since I had seen my old college roommate James, but he hadn't changed much. Will, at least he hadn't changed much physically. But, I was about to find out how much his life had changed since we were rooming together in college.

I ran into James at the 15th reunion of our college class. He looked good, he had shorter hair and had added more muscle to his still very athletic frame, but he was still the James that I remembered. We soon got into talking about what we had done since we graduated. I had become a writer and I worked for a New York Magazine, and he was a self-made millionaire businessman who now lived in Chicago.

We had been more than just roommates in college, we were not lovers, but more like friends with benefits, or just plain fuck buddies. We talked for hours about the things that we had done and the hunky guys we had fucked in our college dorm room.

When we started to talk about the present, I quickly started to see how much our lives had changed since our crazy college days. I had a regular career and a long-term lover and James had become a leather master, who owned his own slave. The whole thing did not startle me in least, in our college days James had always been a real bossy young man.

When I asked about what it was like to own a man slave James did not say a word, he just smiled and then said, "Well Mr. Writer, if you want to know about my slave you will just have to come to Chicago and interview him. That's if you have the nerve? James was still playing, "I dare you James," just like back in our college days. So, naturally I just had to call his bluff. That is how I ended up doing an interview with a gay man slave, something that I had never dreamed that I would someday do.

To get ready for the interview I did as I had always done a lot of research. Before I write about something, I like to know my subject. But, this subject, I soon found out could not be nailed down and defined as most subjects that I had researched. There were some basic standards involved in such relationships, but they were not written in concrete. The individual masters and slaves sort of made up their own rules and terms for such relationships.

At the end of my research I was left with nothing more than just a public image of what a gay master/slave relationship was, that is the general gay image. Would this general image stand up to reality?

What sort of image is that? Will the general picture that most non-leather community gays have of such relationships is that the master is usually a very dominate, sometimes sadistic man, who is better educated and more financially successful than his slave. The slave in the property of his master and the master can do whatever he wants with his property and the slave is usually a person who is burned out on life. He is not well educated, if he works he makes low wages, he has a low self-image and he is not usually a great looking physical specimen. Was this viewpoint valid; well at least was it valid in the case of James and his man slave?

I arrived in Chicago on a windy, fairly cold, weekend in late April. James had given me his address. It was an address of a townhouse on the Gold Coast area of Chicago. James, it seemed, lived in a very high priced area of the city.

When I knocked on the door, James answered the door. "Hi Brad, let me take your coat."

"I thought that you had a slave to open doors and take people's coats?"

"I do, but my boy is out doing some shopping. I did not expect you for another hour."

"As I sat down in the living room of what had to be a very expensive two-story, brownstone, townhouse, I heard the front door open. James than walked into the kitchen area and I could hear him say, "Boy, put that stuff away and strip, I will introduce you to the man who will interview you."

"Yes Sir!"

I wasn't prepared for the next scene in this little drama. After sitting quietly with James for a moment, hearing the opening and closing of cabinet doors and then the sound of clothes being taken off, the person described as "Boy" walked into the room buck-naked. The 'Boy' was wearing only a slave chain around his neck, as he proceeded to stand submissively in front of me with his hands behind his back with his head bowed.

The Boy was quiet a physical specimen, not at all what I had expected. James, at this point was smiling at me, just before he proudly said, "Well, Brad would you like to inspect my property?" I didn't know what to say I just nodded in agreement and got up and started to inspect James's man slave.

The "Boy," was a blond, smooth bodied, super hung, pretty boy. He was not at all what I believe anyone would have expected to be a well-trained man slave. He was about 5'8" tall, a probably weighed about 150 pounds. His body was very muscular and well-defined, as if I had spent a lot of time in a gym and he had been on a rigid diet of some sort. As I ran my hands over his naked body, he started to moan a little. He was really enjoying the touch of my hands on his bare skin.

The two major points of interest were his cock and ass. As I started to fondle his firm, hairless balls, his big cock (9+ fat inches) sprang to rigid attention. His ass way a perfect bubble butt and as I ran my fingers along the crack of his beautiful ass, his body started to tense-up and mildly shake. He had very good physical reactions to being touched.

As I sat down again James just had to ask, "Well Brad, what do you think of my property?"

"James, all I can say is he is not what I expected. How did you ever find and manage to train a young, well-hung, blond pretty boy? Such young men are usually out in some bar dancing there asses off and prick-teasing guys like me."

"It's a long story and I will let my slave tell it to you. I will leave you two alone. I have to go to a meeting down town. I will be back in about 3 hours. Well Brad, he is yours, ask him any questions that you want to and if you want to have him please you he is yours until tomorrow morning." James than picked up his coat and walked out of the apartment. I was left sitting silently in my chair with a naked, pretty boy slave, standing in front of me with a throbbing hard-on.

I know enough from my research about handling a slave to at least get through an interview. Why should I be uptight, he was there to please me. "Get on your knees Boy!"

"Yes Sir!"

WHAT IS YOUR NAME?

"It is Boy Sir! But it was formerly Robert."

WHY WAS YOUR NAME CHANGED?

"After I sold myself to my master, he decided that he wanted to just call me Boy. That is my name now Sir."

HOW OLD ARE YOU?

"I'm 23 years old Sir!"

HOW MUCH FORMAL EDUCATION DO YOU HAVE?

"Because of my master's help I recently finished my college degree in Economics Sir!"

DO YOU WORK OUTSIDE OF YOUR MASTER'S HOUSEHOLD?

"No Sir! I am a house slave. My master does not want, nor need me to work outside his household. My job is to keep care of my master's property and to please him in any way that he wants me to."

DO YOU LIKE YOUR JOB?

"Yes Sir! I can't imagine a better life for me than in serving my master. To me he is like a God."

I just nodded in agreement. James was quiet a good-looking stud.

HOW DID YOU MEET YOUR MASTER?

"I first saw him at a leather bar about two years ago. He just stood out from the crowd. I just could not take my eyes off of him. I asked some other leather men who he was and they filled me in. I was happy to find out that he fit the description of the type of man who I dreamed of serving. He was good-looking, successful, well-educated, wealthy and a real stud. But, at the time, I didn't have the nerve to approach him since he had paid not real attention to me. Most leather men did not pay much attention to me. They would take one look at me and think I was just another pretty boy out for a night in a leather bar and that is all."

"When my master started to leave the bar I noticed that he was wearing a black handkerchief in his left back pocket of his faded jeans. It told me that he was a possible master and I followed him out of the bar. Half way down the block, he noticed that I was following him and he stopped and turned around and gave me a hard stare. I knew that because I did not look the part of a submissive I would have to prove myself, so I quickly got on my knees and said, Please Sir! May I serve and please you?"

"He did not speak at first he just silently walked around me. Finally, he spoke. Get up your feet Boy! Yes Sir! When I was on my feet, he did something unexpected, he slapped me really hard, twice. The blows almost knocked me off my feet. As I regained my footing I said repeated, "Please Sir! May I serve and please you?" He did not speak for almost five more minutes. Finally, he grabbed me by my collar, pulled my face up to his, and said, "So, Boy you want to serve and please." Yes Sir, I will do anything that you want. "Boy you don't look the part, but I am in the mood to give you a chance." Thank you Sir! "Follow me Boy!"

"He took me to a brown stone house that he owned and he really put me through the paces. All through the rest of the night he whipped, man handled and slapped me around, royally fucked me and had me service his cock repeatedly. I had never been so completely used and abused by a top in my whole life. By the time the sun came up I know that I had found the master I wanted. The only question was did he want me?"

DID HE WANT YOU?

"Yes Sir! I had really impressed him. I stayed with him for a month before he enslaved me and made me his property. That was the best day of my life.

DID YOUR MASTER THAN TRAIN YOU TO SERVE HIM?

"No Sir, he did not have the time to really train a slave. He is a very busy businessman. He sent me to a slave trainer that he knew and trusted. My training master owned a ranch in New Mexico. I spent 6 months learning how to be a total slave. A slave my master would be proud to own.

DID YOU SIGN A CONTRACT WHEN YOU WERE ENSLAVED?

"Yes Sir! It was a standard slave contract with certain restrictions and benefits."

WHAT TYPE OF RESTRICTIONS?

"Things like my master cannot brand, sexually alter, permanently shave my body, tattoo me, and pierce any part of my body without written permission from me.

WHAT ARE THE BENEFITS?

"My master will see to it that I am properly trained to serve a master that I am kept in good physical condition and I will be never asked to do anything that is dangerous or unlawful. Also, my master promised to pay me a small salary of $1,000 dollars a month for managing his household. He calls it my walking around money. He also puts $50,000 dollars a year into a trust that is under my control. The money is invested by me in stocks of small developing companies in the energy, high tech and bio-tech fields. My master gives me his expert advice on what stocks to buy. Thanks to my master's help, my trust is growing very rapidly in value. The trust is to provide me with financial security for the future. My master keeps very good care of me. I am a very lucky slave."

I just smiled. Trust James, the professional businessman, to come up with a win-win situation for even a master/slave relationship. Not that he is being overly generous. He is getting this well-trained, very devoted man slave for about what a wealthy man like him would pay an experienced butler.

IS YOUR SLAVE CONTRACT FOR LIFE?

"No Sir! It is for a ten year period."

CAN YOU END YOUR SLAVE CONTRACT AT ANY TIME AND JUST WALK AWAY WITH YOUR TRUST FUND?

"Yes and no, Sir! Only my master can end my contract. But, if it did end before the 10 years ran out I could still manage the trust, but I could not touch the money until the full 10 years were up."

Trust James to put such a clause in a slave contract. This angle will keep his slave loyal for the full ten years.

CAN YOUR MASTER SELL YOU IF HE WANTS TO?

"Yes Sir! If my master decides that he does not want me anymore, he has the right to sell me for the remaining time of my contract. My new master would be bound to the terms of the contract. I would have no trouble with it if he wanted to sell me. It is his right. But, I am one hell of a good slave and my master has said that I am his most valuable property, so I don't see any chance that he would want to sell me."

I nodded my head in agreement. I can't figure out any reason that James would have for selling such a property either.

DOES YOUR MASTER WHIP OR PUNISH YOU A LOT?

"At first my master would punish me a lot, but I am now a well-trained slave. My master seldom has to punish me now. My master whips me when he is putting on some type of show for other leather masters, but he seldom whips me for his own pleasure. I wish he would whip me more I have come to really enjoy the feel of a good whipping by an expert. Pain tends to turn me on and make my dick hard."

This slave may look like a pretty boy, but in fact, he is a stone cold masochist.

DO YOU SLEEP AT THE FOOT OF YOUR MASTER'S BED?

"Occasionally, I sleep on the floor at the foot of my master's bed when my master is not feeling well, but most of the time I sleep with my master, which I enjoy very much."

IS THERE ANYTHING ABOUT YOUR MASTER THAT YOU WOULD LIKE TO SEE CHANGED?

"No Sir! He is perfect for me. I worship him. I would be lost without him in my life."

At this point I decided to end the interview, just looking at this well-developed, man slave was starting to really turn me on. It was time to test drive this slave and see what he is made of.

"Boy, does your master have any toys that he uses on you, such as whips and handcuffs etc.?"

"Yes Sir! He has quite a few such toys. I can get you any toys that you want to use on me Sir!"

The boy was smiling a little. He was eager to play.

"Boy, go get a whip, some body oil, cuffs and some nipple clamps."

"Yes Sir!"

As the slave walked into an area in the back of the apartment I stripped off all of my clothes except my boxer shorts and then sat down in one of the high back leather chairs.

After the slave returned with the items that I wanted I stood up and ordered him to open his mouth. I put my half-hard cock into his mouth and said, "Slave I have some piss for you." I emptied my bladder down his eager throat. He swallowed every drop.

"Slave, now start licking my feet." As he bent down to lick my feet, I bent over and ran my hands down his back, until I started to slap his bare ass really hard. His body tensed up and he moaned a little.

After he had done a good job of licking my feet, I backed away and dropped my shorts, exposing my now throbbing hard cock. I grabbed my cock and pulled it back to my waist. "O.K. Boy, lick my balls."

"Yes Sir!"

The feel of his hot, moist tongue massaging my balls caused my legs to shake and I grit my teeth. "Slave, suck my cock." He smiled a little. "Yes Sir!" He swallowed my big cock like he was a hungry dog. The feel of my cock sliding down his warm, wet throat caused my body to mildly shake.

It only took a few minutes of his expert cock sucking to get me to the point of climax. As my cock swelled up, I let out a loud moan as I grabbed the back of his head and shoved my cock down his throat. After he had swallowed the last drops of my cum, he started to slowly lick the remaining cum off of my still hard and throbbing cock.

It was time to see how much pain this pretty boy could take. I ordered him to grab the molding at the top of a doorway that led into the kitchen. I pick out a nice cat of nine tales from the pile of toys that he had brought back.

As he waited, I walked over to him and ran my hands over his naked body, occasionally stopping to twist his nipples, or squeeze his balls really hard, causing him to moan and his body to shake.

As the first strike of my whip hit his bare ass, his body tensed up and he stood for a moment on his tiptoes. As I continued to whip his ass, back and the back of his legs, slowly building up power of each strike, his body began to violently shake and his moans grew louder.

After his backside had a nice light pink glow, I stopped for a minute and walked up to him and started to rub my hands over his naked body as I dry fucked his ass cheeks. He started to move his ass with the motion of my cock, he was really enjoying this.

After I applied a thin coat of oil to his backside, I started to whip him with more force. The oil will make sure that I didn't leave any lasting marks on him. After only a few minutes, he started to scream and violently squirm, but he never took his hands off the top of the door and his cock stayed rock hard. This was a sure sign that he was in fact really enjoying this whipping.

With his backside now a nice red color, I cleaned his back off with a towel and then I grabbed him by the hair on the back of his head and I led him into the bedroom and proceeded to fuck his pretty ass for the next hour or so. When I was done with him, I rewarded him by letting him cum.

I awoke the next morning to an empty bed. Confused I quickly sat up and then noticed that James's slave was kneeling naked on the floor. I got up and walked over and played with hair on his head as he said, "Sir did I please you last night?" I smiled. "Yes Boy you were a pleasure to work with last night."

"Thank you Sir!"

The plane flight home was relaxing. Man that was one hell of a head-trip. After all of those times that pretty boys had prick teased me it felt really good to humiliate, whip and royally fuck the shit out of a drop dead gorgeous pretty boy. You could say that it was even therapeutic. God, if I could only train my lover to be half as interesting as James's slave.

CHAPTER THREE

LOCKER ROOM LUST

PUBLISHED IN MANDATE MAGAZINE: SEPTEMBER 2006

Man, I have the best job a young gay guy in college could ever dream of having. Well, in my opinion it is a dream job. It not only helps to pay my bills but it is the biggest sexual turn on in my college boy life. What sort of college job could be such a big sexual turn on? Well, I'm the assistant equipment room manager for the college football team.

What's the big sexual turn on, it's the team. Most of the team will rate high on the sex appeal score board, but several of them are drop dead gorgeous and I get to see them walk pass my equipment booth buck naked several times a week. If they knew what I dream about doing to their naked bodies, they would blush several shades of red.

I've had this job for almost a year. I have bonded so well with the team that they have given me a knick name, "Little Bro." I guess it is because I am the shortest person in the locker room.

I'm only 5'8" tall and weigh only 150 pounds. Next to these guys, I don't show up much.

My job is basically to hand out and take in equipment and uniforms and to do the laundry. Before a game, I hand out the uniforms and equipment to the players and when the game is over they return all that stuff to me. Sometimes return is not the right word. At times they just bury me under it as they file into the shower room. Being buried under a football teams sweaty, smelly uniforms can be a strangely erotic experience.

Everything about my life has been very low key and predictable, but I was soon to learn that my life was about to take a radical and very interesting turn because of a simple thing like a rainstorm. A sudden, heavy rainstorm really soaked me good during one of our at home games. I was dripping wet when the team dumped their muddy, wet uniforms all over me, as they usually do, which of course did not help my appearance any. The equipment room manager took one look at me and told me to strip and go take a shower with the team while he handled the laundry. Man, I didn't need to be told twice; I was naked and heading for the showers in less than a minute.

While I had been staring at the guys on the team when they were naked for some time none of them had ever seen me in the nude. As I walked into the shower room, several of the team members looked a little startled. But, the shock of seeing me naked quickly wore off.

After I finished showering I grabbed a towel to dry off, I noticed that for once some of the team members were staring at my naked body. I was surprised to see that Jack, the team's star quarterback, acted very interested in me. To be more exact he seemed very interested in my ass. I have what some people would call a nice looking, hairless, bubble butt.

Jack is the stuff of gay dreams. He is a 6'2" tall, dark haired, good looking, young stud and he weighs in with about 200 pounds of solid, gym-toned muscle. This whole package is well accented by a nice, firm, rounded ass and about a 9-inch man cock. The team members call him cowboy, because he was raised on a ranch and he always wears cowboy boots.

After the team had gotten dressed and left the building, I closed up the equipment room, turned off the air conditioning and started to walk out of the empty locker room. Well, at least I thought that I was the only one there.

As I started to open the front door of the locker room, I felt a hand on my shoulder. Startled, I quickly turned around to stand face to face with Jack. I swallowed hard. I did not know what to expect.

Jack squeezed my shoulder and smiled, "Hey Little Bro, that was some show that you put on in the shower room today." I just stood there starting into Jack's deep blue eyes. I didn't know what to say.

"You know, showing off that nice body and great looking ass of yours." My body started to relax now it seems that I wasn't in any type of trouble. "Well yes, I guess I have a good body." Jack just smiled and said, "Well, take it from me you have a lot going for you." Jack now squeezed one of my ass cheeks and said, "Little Bro have you even had those nice buns cream filled?"

The mystery of the moment was gone. It was now very obvious that Jack was aching to fuck me, which was an idea that really starting to turn me on. Somehow, I got up the nerve to say, "What do you have in mind Jack?"

"You know people don't call me "Cowboy" just because I wear cowboy boots. Once in a while I like to get in the saddle and go for a ride, if you know what I mean. Jack now grabbed my ass with both hands and pulled me up against his big chest.

I just had to ask him. "Well do I get some hot foreplay or do you just intend to fuck me right here and now." Jack smiled, he had me and he knew it. "Oh, I want to fuck you alright, but we can do it any way that you want." This was the opening I wanted. I smiled and then walked over and open the door to the mat room and said, "Well cowboy, the first one who gets buck naked calls the shots." It was no contest. I was standing naked in front of him and sporting a throbbing hard-on before he was half-undressed.

Just after he dropped his shorts I put my hands on his shoulders and gently pushed him backward and had him sit down, one foot on each side, on a rounded up wrestling mat and then I sat on his lap. With Jack holding on to my bare ass with both of his hands and our now hard cocks up against each other, I put my arms around his neck, leaned forward and gave him a long, slow, wet kiss. That first kiss progressed into about 15 minutes of making out that soon had me breathing rapidly and my cock throbbing so hard that it started to hurt.

The temperature in the mat room was rapidly rising and beads of sweat were starting to form on our naked bodies. As I kissed my way up and down both sides of Jack's neck, he started to run his fingers down my back until he was gently caressed the crack of my ass. The light touch of his fingers caused my body to mildly shake.

Now, I was ready to work on the rest of what had only been my dreams up to now. I stood up and slowly pushed Jack backwards, so that he was lying on his back on the rolled up mat.

Looking down at Jack's sweat covered, extremely hot naked body was enough to get a horny gay guy like me to cum, right then and there, but I had better ideas. I leaned down and started to lick and kiss his shoulders, before proceeding down his body. I lifted up his arms and licked each of his armpits before working on his nipples. Jack was really enjoying my little performance. At times his body would shake and he would softly say things like, "Damn, that feels good and Yes, Yes, Yes." All of which just encouraged me to work harder.

Finally, I got to what I had only dreamed about doing up to now. I kissed my way down his torso until I was licking his big, firm balls. The first time my warm, wet tongue touched Jack's balls his body jerked. After I had given his balls a nice warm bath, I licked my way up his throbbing cock until my tongue was massaging the head of his dick.

In one fast movement, I swallowed his big cock as far down my throat as I could. Jack let out a loud moan and his body shook. What happened next was a big surprise. Just after I had deep throated Jack's cock just a few times his body started to shake and he grabbed my head and forced his cock down my throat, just before I felt his big cock swell up and unload several shots of warm, sweet cum down my throat.

After his cock relaxed, I started to lick the remaining cum off of his still hard and pulsating cock as Jack's body mildly squirmed.

When I was finished, I stood up, looked down at Jack, and said, "God, you are horny." Jack only laid there and smiled. "Now, cowboy it is your turn."

When Jack's breathing had returned to normal he sat up, put his hands on my bare ass, and pulled my body toward him. It was now his turn to please me. He started by tongue massaging my nipples, one at a time, as his finger continued to lightly massage my back and my ass. The more that I moaned and shook the more turned-on Jack seemed to get. His still hard cock was pulsating up and down like he was a dog in heat.

He then started to gently lower my body, down on to the mat as he started to kiss and tongue his way down my chest and stomach until he raised my legs up and spread my ass cheeks.

When his warm, wet tongue started to massage my hole, my muscles tensed up.

For the next few minutes, I just enjoyed the feel of his warm, wet tongue massage my asshole as his hands gently caressed my legs. My body was totally relaxed by the time he stopped and I felt the pressure of a big, spit covered cock, slowly slid deep into my ass. My body quickly adjusted to the feel of a big man cock sliding in and out of my hungry ass and I began to really enjoy the feel of being royally fucked.

I now started to move my hips up and down as thrusts of Jacks big cock started to pick up speed. In only a few minutes, I was moaning and shaking as Jacks buried his cock deeper and deeper into me. Without air conditioning, the temperate in the mat room had become more like a sauna. With each thrust of Jack's big cock I moaned and my body slid a little bit forward on the now sweat covered wrestling mat.

Next, Jack rolled me up on my side in a fetal position and he started to fuck me sideways until I again started to moan. Whenever I started to loudly moan and my body started to shake Jack would stop fucking me and he would lean forward and start to lick beads of sweat off of my neck and face. Jack had quickly learned how to play my body like a find tuned musical instrument.

After fucking me in several different sexual positions, Jack put me on my back with my legs on his shoulders. As he fucked me, his hands lightly caressed the sides of my legs as he slowly tongue massaged my feet. The whole scene quickly started to drive me crazy.

The more I moaned and my body shook the faster Jack shoved his big cock into me. I could see it on his face he wasn't going to stop me this time.

My body started to get rigid. I could feel the erotic tension rise in my groin and I moaned so loud I almost screamed. Just after my cock erupted Jack's body tensed-up and he shot his load up my ass. After I had shot my last stream of warm, sticky cum all over my chest and waist I looked up at Jack, he was still breathing hard, sweat was pouring off his upper body and steams of cum were dripping down his still hard and throbbing cock. I had only one thought on my mind. God, he is one fucking beautiful hunk of man.

He smiled, leaned over and kissed me. "Wow, you are one hell of a good ride." He then got up and lifted me off of the mat and held me against his sweat covered, naked body and ran his hands down my back until his had a firm grip on my ass cheeks. "Little Bro, you are really incredible sex. I just hope that you will let this cowboy take some more rides in the near future.

I put my hand behind his neck, I pulled his head down, and I gave him a deep kiss before I looked into his eyes and said, "Cowboy you can ride me any time that you want."

CHAPTER FOUR

TRAINING

I will always remember the date. It March the 17th day of the year 2034. This was the day my uncle and guardian sold me into slavery. Just after my eighteenth birthday, my uncle Bert, an oil field employee, of an American firm, in the Middle East, told me to get packed. He said to me, "Boy, you are going to be enrolled in a trade school. I am tired of supporting your gay ass." My uncle had found out three months ago that I was gay and he made it plain that he did not like gay people. In short, my life of living with my uncle had become a living hell.

The trade school it turned out was in the country of Morocco, North Africa. After we landed in Morocco, my uncle rented a car and we drove out into the desert. As we approached our destination, my uncle stopped the car for a moment in the middle of the desert.

My uncle pointed his finger at me, a bad sign, and he said, "Boy, due the fact that you have no employable skills, let alone a real trade. I will be enrolling you in the only trade in which you could possibly make a living at. Your only real asset is your pretty body and big cock. So, I have decided to make use of your main assets to get you a job that I think you can handle."

"Boy, I have decided and I have arranged to sell you into slavery. Selling you will enable me to regroup the money I have wasted on raising your gay ass during the last four years. Now this is how it is going to be. When we meet the head man of this organization and he inspects you. You are to agree that I have the right to sell you. If you fuck up this sale, I will handcuff you and we will walk far out into the desert. You will not be coming back with me. Do you understand Boy?"

There was nothing that I could say that would change my uncle's mine. Complaining, bitching and crying would have no effect on my uncle. Once he has made up his mind that is it.

"Yes Sir." What else could I say? My uncle is a big powerful and brutal man. If he wanted to kill me with his bare hands, he could.

When we drive up to an old fortress like building in an oasis. My uncle ordered me out of the car. I was then ordered to strip off all of my clothes. After I was naked, I was told to follow two men, who were dressed like soldiers, into the fortress like building. My uncle followed us.

I was led into a big, almost empty room. An older man, dressed in a very expensive business suit, with the look of authority about him, walked up to me and started to visually inspect my naked body. He seemed to be very impressed. The man than ordered me not to move. He then started physically inspected every inch of my body, sometimes in a very brutal manner.

This man, who seems to be in charge, than asked me to respond to some questions. I said, "Yes Sir.'

"Boy, does your uncle have the right to sell you to me." I tried not to look startled. "Yes, Sir, he has that right."

"Boy why does a very pretty young man like you want to be a slave?" This was the moment of truth that my uncle was afraid of. I could feel my uncle's eyes on the back of my neck. If I get this answer wrong, I will be dead in no more than an hour.

"Sir, I have known from the time that I was only twelve years old that my destiny was to kneel naked at the feet of my master. That is why god has given me such a beautiful body. It will enable me to better please my master, Sir."

The man smiled and then he motioned to my uncle to come forward. They talked for a few minutes and then they shook hands. Some papers were signed and the deal was approved. That was it. I was now a slave and I now belonged to this strange man.

My uncle was paid in gold coins. I counted them as they were given to my uncle. I had been sold into slavery for the price of 40 gold coins. My uncle smiled and shook the man's hand. Then he left the room. My new master ordered me to kneel on the floor, to be quiet, and not to move. He then walked out of the room and turned off the lights. About thirty minutes later the lights went back on, two soldiers walked in and grabbed me by both my arms, marched me out of the room and down a long hallway to a room full of large pillows. I was thrown on to the pillows and ordered to lay face down. I obeyed.

In a few minutes, I heard about a dozen people walk into the room. A voice rang out in English that simply said, "Boy, do not move." Just after the men surrounded me and I felt that sting of a whip on my back. For the next half hour, the soldiers took turns at whipping my backside with a light whip.

The whipping was painful, but it did not break my skin. That was just the first round. When the soldiers were through whipping me, they all took a turn in raping my ass.

When they were done gang raping me they all pissed on me as I laid on the cold stone floor. They then left the room. I did not know what to do. I could not think straight. So, I just decided not to move until I was told to move.

All I could think was, "Oh God is this the way the rest of my life was going to be like. The thought scared the hell out of me.

My silence only lasted a few minutes. Than an old lady appeared and indicated that I was to follow her. She led me to a crude, run down bathroom. I was allowed to use the toilet and then she washed my piss-covered body with a wet sponge, as she played with my balls and ass.

After being cleaned up two guards led me to a cell like room that had only a cot like bed, one chair and a table in it. The guards shackled my legs to a ring in the back wall and I was told, in fairly good English to get some sleep.

Early the next morning, just after sunrise, I was awakened by the feel of someone ripping the covers off me. Startled, I looked up to see a man in a military uniform bending over me. "Sit up Boy!"

"Yes Sir." The man now unlocked the shackles on my ankles. "Stand up Boy!" I quickly got to my feet, bowed my head and put my hands behind my back. "Boy step forward two steps."

"Yes Sir!" I took two steps forward and stood submissively waiting for my next order. The early morning sunlight was shining though the small window in the room directly on my naked body.

The man just silently stared at me for several minutes, before speaking. "Boy, I'm glad to see that you at least have a basic knowledge of how to act in the presence of your superiors. We are getting off to a good start.

My name is Colonel Caffa and I am a retired officer of the French Foreign Legion. I have been hired to train you for the next 6 months, to be a total slave. I will train you to be a slave that any real master would be proud to own.

"During your training I will be your master, your training master. I own you and you will do anything that I say. Pleasing me will become the focus of your life. You will exist only to serve and please me, your master. Nothing else will matter to you. Do you understand what I am saying Boy!"

"Yes Sir!"

"While I am training you, you will address me as Sir! You will only speak when I ask you a question. When you have permission to speak, you will end each sentence with Sir! Do you understand me Boy?"

"Yes Sir!"

"Now Boy prepared to be inspected, put your hands at your side and stare straight ahead."

"Yes Sir!"

"Now Boy I don't know much about you at present, but I am going to find out a few things right now." To start my inspection my new master silently walked around me several times visually inspecting my naked body. After he seemed satisfied, he started to physically inspect me starting with my teeth and proceeding down my naked body, probing, grabbing, slapping and tickling every square inch of me, until he had inspected my feet. I was now told to spread my legs and bend over. "Yes Sir!" As I bent over my master started to lightly massage the crack of my ass, which caused my body to squirm and shake. I than felt several wet fingers slid into my ass and start to probe and massage my prostate gland. My cock got throbbing hard and I started to moan. As my master withdrew his fingers, my body relaxed and I was ordered to stand up.

My master seemed to be done with his physical inspection of my body, but I was soon to learn that he was not done with me. "Boy, raise your arms and put your hands behind your head."

"Yes Sir!"

My master walked out of the room. In a few minutes, he came back with a whip in his hands. It looked like the same whip that had been used on me the night before. My master walked around to stand behind me and I closed my eyes and waited to feel the sting of the whip. The first strike of the whip landed on my bare ass and my body tensed up. As blows fell on my back, ass and then the back of my legs, I gritted my teeth and my body began to squirm.

Suddenly, after about 10 minutes of whipping, my master stopped and he just stood behind me and didn't say a thing. After a few minutes of silently standing, with my hands behind my head, my master walked around to stand in front of me. The first blow hit my chest and then my waist and finally the front of my legs. For the next 10 to 15 minutes my master lightly whipped both the front and back of my naked body. When my master was done, he put the whip on the dresser and he told me to put my arms down and to stand submissively again. As my master walked around me physically inspecting the damage of his whipping, my whole body could still feel the sting of the whip. A mild pain pulsated though out my body.

"Well Boy, I am finding out a lot about you today. You have a great body, good bodily reactions and you can handle a good deal of pain. Most masters would find you to be very entertaining and that is good. A slave only exists to please his master."

"Now Boy, get on your knees in the proper position for a slave. "Yes Sir!" I dropped to my knees, put my hands behind my back and bowed my head. "Now Boy, I will explain what I intend to do with you these next 6 months. I will start by breaking you just like a cowboy would break a wild horse and then I will remold you, in mind and body to be a total slave. You will forget all that stuff about having rights and being treated fairly. You will learn that you are a slave and that you exist only to serve and please your master. Your life will have no other meaning. Now Boy, repeat after me, *I am a slave.*"

"I am a slave."

"I exist only to please and serve my master."

"I exist only to please and serve my master."

"Repeat what you have just said, over and over, until I tell you to stop."

"Yes Sir!"

"I am a slave. I exist only to serve and please my master. I am a sl–."

My master had me repeat the words, over and over again, for the next 15 minutes. When I was ordered to stop, my master said, "Boy you are only saying the words today, but at the end of your training you will believe every word that you say. When I am though training you, you will know that you are a slave and your whole life will be focused on serving and pleasing your master."

"Do you understand Boy?"

"Yes Sir, I understand Sir!" This routine became part of my training program. Every day I was required to kneel naked on the floor and repeat, over and over again for a 15 minutes a day that, "I am a slave. I exist only to serve and please my master."

My new master seemed satisfied with me, so far. He left the room again for several minutes. When he returned, he locked a metal collar around my neck. "Boy, this is your slave collar. It is an electronic, high tech device that let me know where you are at all times. It is waterproof, shockproof, knife proof and tamperproof. It is indestructible.

So if you ever have any stupid ideas about escaping, forget them. You are a slave for the next 5 years. Do you understand what I have just said Slave!"

"Yes Sir!

After only a few hours in the fortress with my new master, he had me put on a light cotton robe and some sandals. I was only told that we were going for a ride.

I followed my new master out to his vehicle, a British Range rover. During the drive, all I could think of was maybe things will work out for the better and I will be sold to a kind master.

My master took me to his home, near a small military base, in an isolated area. My master's house was to be my home for the next 6 months. The house was a stone and wood two-story structure that looked like it had been well cared for. That night I slept at the foot of my master's bed. My first duty in the morning was sucking off my new master, which was a job that I really liked. My new master was a man who was in his late 40's, but he was in great physical shape. He was about 6'2" in height and I would say he weighed a little over 200 pounds. He was a ruggedly good-looking man. I learned to really enjoy the times that he rewarded me by letting me please his cock. It got so that I dreamed about those moments.

My first few days of training were spent in learning my household duties and in telling my master all about my past life. I knelt submissively at my master's feet for hours telling him every detail of my past life. He showed a great deal of interest in the years that I spent living with my two daddies. He said that being a daddy's boy was good for me it made me easier to train as a slave. In my master's opinion, being a good daddy's boy had half way trained my mind to be a good man slave. It was during these first few days of training that I started to see that my master was a strict, but fair man.

After only a short week my master had trained me in how to manage his house and he knew all he wanted to know about me. Now my physically and mental training would begin. My master got up at sunrise and he expected me to be awake and knelling naked at the foot of his bed. After we showered and I cared for any sexual needs my master may have, I prepared the first meal of the day.

When my master had finished his meal, I was allowed 20 minutes to eat and then I was to wash the dishes and put everything away. After eating his meal my master liked to read for about an hour in the living room. When I was done with cleaning up after the first meal of the day I was expected to go into the living room, kneel by my master's chair, and wait for him to have something for me to do.

After my master was though reading he would order me to put on my running clothes and we would join the Moroccan Army soldiers, from the nearby army base, for a several mile run though the local foothills. My master did not think much of the Moroccan Army. "Boy the Moroccan Army is nothing but shit. They are not a real fighting force. They are only good for parades. I would never depend on them to help me in a military situation. But, they are good for some things like running."

After running, it was time for mental training. At times my master would have me do stupid things like pick up a large rock and take it down and up a hill and then bring it back down again, over and over. This was to train me to not think about what I was told to do, but just to focus on doing the task as well as I could.

Yoga was part of my mental training. My master said, "Boy you have to know how to control your body and mind. Sometimes your master will have no use for you and you will be required to stand or kneel for long periods of time and you have to know how to mentally and physically handle such an inactive state." I was also told that a slave that can handle such a situation and will earn his master's respect.

The second week of my training my master added massage to my program. Once a week a professional masseur would give me lessons in massage. Mr. Leon was a friend of my master and he had been hired to teach me the art of massage. My master believed that a good man slave needed to know how to give his master a full body massage.

Mr. Leon was an expert masseur and I learned a lot from him. He was also good for other things. Mr. Leon was paid in two ways for his services. He was paid for his lessons and he was allowed to use me for his pleasure after the lessons. I soon found out that my teacher was a hard-core top man and he made good use of my pretty slave ass. It seems that he liked my ass so much that he convinced my master that I could use two lessons per week. I became a better masseur each week and my pretty ass got a good workout too.

In mid-morning, I was required to fix and serve the second meal of the day. After I had cleaned up after the meal, I returned to kneeling naked by my master's chair. An hour after the noon day meal my master took me to work out in his own home gym. The gym was in a large room in the basement of my master's home. It was very well outfitted and my master really put me through my paces. His goal was to change my boyish body to a muscular man's body. He told me he was going to add 30 pounds of defined muscle to my frame in the next 6 months. I really liked the idea of building up my body.

My master was a strict taskmaster those first few months. I wasn't able to always do as he said and he would whip me, but slowly I developed as he wanted me to and he seldom had to use his whip on me. Physically and mentally, I was starting to settle into the role of a well-trained man slave.

My master would at times show that he recognized that I had made good progress and he would complement me or reward me by letting me cum. Sometimes my master would not let me cum for a full month. He was of the opinion that a horny slave will serve his master best. He was right of course, he was always right. I did put more effort into my duties and training when I was horny.

Even the pleasure of cumming was turned into a training period. Each time I was allowed to cum my master tried to train me mentally to cum without touching myself. I was told that if I succeeded in getting off by using my mind I would be rewarded. The first time that I was able to do it my master gave me the reward that I wanted; he fucked me for two hours straight. My master may be middle aged, but his big cock works as good as any young man.

My training program did not remain the same. When I would reach a goal that my master set for me, another stage in my training would open up. After several months of training one interesting change was made in my training program, it concerned sex. The change involved the use of the Moroccan soldiers.

My master had no use for the Moroccan soldiers as a fighting force, but he did have a use for them in my training program. My master was very close to the officer who commanded the soldiers in the camp next to his home. He had served Morocco as an officer in the Legion and he had many connections in the Moroccan Army. He used his influence to get the use of some of the Moroccan soldiers to help train me.

The Moroccan soldiers knew that I was the colonel's slave and from the looks in their eyes at different times, I could tell that they wanted to use me for their pleasure. It was a task that I would be eager to perform, so when my master told me that he was going to let the soldiers use me, I thought that I was going to be used to please the soldiers was really starting to turn me on.

Early one morning, during the fourth month of my training, my master told me not to fix the first meal of the day. He said that he had a challenge for me today. I was told to put on a pair of running shoes and nothing else. I quickly did as I was told. My master than handcuffed my hands behind my back and then told me to follow him. I followed my master out of the front door and down the hill to the soldier's camp. I could see that about 30 soldiers were in formation on the parade field and my master headed straight for them. I felt a little nervous at first. I was going to be put on display totally naked in front of a formation of soldiers. I did not know what to expect. I only knew that my master always knew what he was doing and that I would be alright.

When we walked up to the formation, all of the soldiers were staring at me. My master told me to face the soldiers and to bow my head. I did as I was told. When my master bought me out to this field I was very nervous, but the idea of 30 soldiers staring at my naked body had an effect. A surge of sexual energy started to run though my body and my big cock got half-hard. I mentally tried to relax and my cock started to relax.

My master walked, up and down, in front of the soldiers talking in French. Every once in a while he would point at me and some of the soldiers would laugh a little. What was happening I did not know; I did not speak French.

After my master had talked to the soldiers, they went on their morning run, the same early morning run that my master and I usually were part of. My master told me to follow him into one of the barracks. I followed my master into a small room in the back of the building and I was un-cuffed. He ordered me to sit on the floor with my back against the wall and remain silent. I sat down and started to use my mental training to relax my body and mind. As I sat on the floor, my master walked outside and talked to someone in French.

After about an hour my master came back into the room and he put a bath towel on the floor. I was ordered to knell on the towel and my master told me what I was to do. "Boy you are going to be of some use to the Moroccan Army today. You are going to suck off any of the soldiers in this barrack that want their cocks sucked. Do you understand Boy?"

"Yes Sir!"

"And Boy you better do a good job."

I didn't have long to wait before the soldiers returned from their run and started to change out of their sweaty jogging clothes. Each naked soldier walked right past me on their way to the shower room. A line of soldiers quickly formed in front of me. The first soldier was a young man of about 20 years old and he smiled at me as he put his stiff cock in my face. This was probably going to be his first blowjob and I was eager to make him feel good. I swallowed his cock down to the hair in one stroke. The young soldiers moaned and his body shook so much that I though he was going to lose his balance. He only lasted about a minute before he shot his load down my throat.

The second soldier was just a teenager. He probably was 18 years old or so, he had red hair and a very pretty 9-inch cock that was already hard and throbbing. He held me by the back of my head as I sucked his cock. He was like the first soldier. He was so horny that he got off really fast. The taste of warn, sweet cum flowing down my throat had my big cock throbbing like crazy.

Most of the soldiers were so horny that it was easy to get them off and none of them gave me any trouble. I was soon horny that I could have sucked them off all day, but after about 20 of them had gotten their rocks off my master called a halt this suck session and I was told to follow my master home. As I walked naked though the barracks many of the soldiers that I had sucked off slapped me on my bare ass. I just smiled and followed my master out the door.

After that day, running with the soldiers was never the same. The soldiers would smile at me and they looked at my ass whenever my master and I ran with them. They had used the colonel's slave and they wanted more. I hoped that my master would reward me again like that, but it is his decision.

I didn't have to wait long for a new challenge that involved the Moroccan soldiers. Several weeks later, my master arranged for me to massage some of the soldiers on a regular basis. He wanted me to get some massage experience.

A massage table was set up in the little room near the showers in the barrack. A bare mattress was also put on the floor of the room. Each massage session was for one hour. I was to massage each soldier for half an hour and then for the next half hour the soldier was allowed to use me for his pleasure if he wanted too. I was eager to tackle this new challenge. The way the soldiers had been looking at and slapping my ass I knew that I was going to get royally fucked.

The first day of my new duty, I went through my regular routine of fixing meals, running with the soldiers, weight training and household duties. In the early afternoon, I was to begin my massage duties. I followed my master's instructions for the sessions. I stripped naked and put on only a pair of running shoes. Wearing only my slave collar and running shoes, I walked out the door of my master's house, down the hill and across the parade field to the barrack. On my way to the barracks, several soldiers looked at my naked body and they started to grab and play with their crotches. They knew that they were finally going to get a chance to fuck me and they looked really eager.

My first client was a stocky sergeant. He walked into the room wearing only a towel. He had just taken a shower. He walked and acted like a man who was used to being in charge. The sergeant took off his towel, exposing a half hard 8-inch cock and he laid face down on the massage table without saying a word. I took this as a sign that he did not speak English.

I gave the soldier a deep tissue massage. The soldier was a perfect subject. No matter how hard I massaged him he did not complain. When the half hour massage was over the sergeant got off the table and looked at my naked body and half smiled. He walked up to me, grabbed me by the hair on the back of my head, and led me over to the mattress on the floor. I was pushed face down onto the mattress and I remained silent and still. The sergeant then started to caress my naked body, until he started to focus on my ass. The sergeant than got up and walked over to my massage table and grabbed a jar of lube. He put a gob of lube on his already hard cock and stroked it several times, as he looked at my pretty ass.

The soldier rode my ass for the next half hour before he shot his load. After he was finished with me, he withdrew and slapped my ass several times and then he got up and walked out of the room. The whole time he was with me, he had not said a thing or shown any form of emotions. He was a real cold fish, but he could really fuck and that is what really mattered to me.

My next client was the 18 year old, red headed soldier with a pretty 9-inch cock. I had sucked him off a few days ago. He walked into the room smiling and he shook my hand. He did not seem to speak much English so I indicated to him that he was to get on the table face down. Massaging him was a pleasure. He was a good-looking young man and he had beautiful smooth skin, a natural body and a great looking ass. The young soldier seemed to like being massaged and he would get playful. At times, when I was massaging him, he would reach out and fondle me, or caress my bare ass. I never tried to stop him I was here to please the soldiers in any way that they wanted me to.

After the massage, the young soldier got off the table and walked right up to me. He grabbed the back of my head and then he kissed me for several minutes, while he fondled me. I couldn't help it but this young man was really turning me on. My big cock was throbbing up and down.

Suddenly, the young man did the unexpected, he walked over to the mattress on the floor and he laid face down. He looked up at me and spoke the only English words that I had heard him speak so far. "Fuck me Sir, fuck me."

I quickly greased my cock, spread his cheeks and started to enter him. He let out a slight moan as my cock slid deep into his ass. I started to take slow deep strokes and the young man started to moan and shake. This young soldier was not a virgin he had been fucked in the past and he liked being a bottom.

I fucked the young soldier for the next half hour, but I did not cum. I did not have my master's permission to cum. After I had withdrawn and gotten to my feet, I bent over and helped the young soldier to get up. After he was on his feet, I looked down at the mattress and noticed that the soldier had shot his load on the mattress. This boy was a born bottom and he really liked being fucked.

The boy was different from the other soldiers and I was to quickly find out how different. As the boy got to his feet, he put his arms around me and gave me a long, deep kiss just before he said in broken English, "You are Colonel's slave and I like that. I would like to be Colonel's slave." With that, he kissed me one more time and then he smiled and left the room.

The third and last client of the day was boring compared to the first two. I ended up sucking him off after the massage and he left the room. The fresh memory of the young red haired soldier made me smile as I cleaned up the room. He was different from the other soldiers, but in a way, he was a lot like me.

As usual, when I got back to my master's house I told him everything that had happen. My master seemed especially interested with what I said about the young red haired soldier.

During my last month of training, I learned that my master was not done in finding interesting ways to use the soldiers to train me. Early one morning my master said, "Boy, you are going on a special diet today. The diet is designed to trim and define your body and get you ready to be sold. For the next two weeks the only things that you are going to have to eat is piss and cum."

"Every day, for the next two weeks, I will take you naked over to the barrack. You will kneel on a bath towel on the floor of the bathroom and twice a day you will suck off the soldiers and also let them piss down your throat. Cum and piss are the only things that you are going to have to eat in the next two weeks. Cum is full of protein and piss is full of vitamins and minerals that the body did not need. Boy, you are going to learn the value of cock. For the next two weeks, cock is going to feed you and keep you alive. Do you understand Boy?"

"Yes Sir!"

So, for the next two weeks I lived off of cock. The first few days were a little rough, but I adjusted to the change and I started to look forward to going to the barrack. Each day I sucked off at least 20 soldiers and had about 10 or 12 soldiers piss down my throat. By the time the two weeks were up, I had lost 14 pounds and my body was so defined that I looked like a road map.

The last two weeks of my training, I was slowly put back on my regular high protein, low carb diet. The energy that I had lost during my special diet came back and I felt great. I was a little startled the first time I looked at myself naked in a mirror.

My master had reached his goal. He had added about 30 pounds of well-defined muscle to my body. I looked like a completely different person. In the mirror, I didn't see the hung boy that I was 6 months before, I saw a very muscular young man. I was starting to look forward to the upcoming auction and I hoped that I would please my master one more time by bringing a high price.

My master had told me the truth that first day at the fortress. He said that he was going to train me to be a total slave and he has succeeded. I no longer feel or think like an average person. I spend every waking minute of my day thinking only of serving and pleasing my master. Nothing else matters to me.

I think my master was right when he told me, "Boy after training you for only 3 months I can already see that you are a natural born submissive. You are a closet slave and I just dragged you out of your closet and made you what you were meant to be, a man's property."

My existence as my master's slave has made me feel very content and safe. I have trouble relating to the work a day world of the average person. I don't have the same worries and concerns of everyday people. I serve my master and he protects and cares for me. I have no worldly problems such as having a career in the business world, paying taxes, caring about what is happening in the world and the local community, or about what other people think. I only care about what my master wants me to do. I feel very content with my new station in life and I see no reason why I would want to change it. I am a slave, the property of my master and that is my life.

CHAPTER FIVE

MAN FEVER

PUBLISHED IN HONCHO MAGAZINE: SEPTEMBER 2005

My moaning grew louder and louder as I started to violently shake, as my man Carlos really started to shove it to me. As I laid face down on the bed, I raised my ass up each time that my man shoved his big ten-inch cock up my ass. I wanted every inch of his huge man cock inside of me.

As my ass started to loosen up, I started to really enjoy the sensation of having the most erotic internal massage of my young life, as my cock started to throb so hard that it started to hurt. I spread my legs out on the mattress in order to tighten up my ass muscles and to intensify the sensation.

My moans grew louder. I was getting close to the point of climax. Carlos seemed to sense the state I was in and he stopped fucking me for a moment while my body relaxed. When my breathing was more normal, Carlos turned me over on my back. He then put my legs on his shoulders and he began to fuck me long and hard again.

After just a few minutes of long, deep strokes, I was starting to build up to climax again. Now, Carlos started to slowly stand up, lifting my ass up in the air, so that I was balancing my body on my shoulders, as he started to fuck me in a downward motion.

God damn it, he was going to do it again? I was going to cum as I watched my own cock throb wildly right above my face. I was soon past the point of no return and my cock unloaded stream after stream of hot, sticky cum, all over my face, just as my man Carlos moaned, tensed up and shoot his load.

As Carlos's body started to relax, he withdrew his big cock and let my body slide down to the mattress. He then handed me a towel to wipe my own cum off my face.

This is one of Carlo's little jokes he liked to see me cream my own face. As a hard-core bottom, who likes super hung guys, I have gotten use to the fact that most heavy hung tops are self-centered jerks.

When I finished cleaning myself up, Carlos was already dressed. "Sorry, I have to go. My wife will be home in about an hour. Thanks for the fuck. You were great." With those words, he was out the door.

Carlos's wife was pregnant. Because of this fact, my hungry ass got royally fucked twice a week by the big stud. It's not a perfect situation, but super hung studs, who really love to fuck, are hard to find. I call Carlos, "My man," but he does not belong to me and never will. This type of situation is par for the course in my life.

You see, I have some sort of curse on me. I dream a lot about dominate, hot and hung studs. You know men who are experienced, heavy hung, good looking, well-educated and know what they want in life. A man who has a mature presence about them, that tells a young man like me that I can depend on and trust him.

O.K. I know, Carlos does not really fill the bill, but up to now, nobody has. A gay guy with a hungry ass like mine has to make do as best he can. Until Mr. Prefect comes along, if he exists at all, I will just have to get fucked by available jerks like Carlos.

So far, my life has worked out O.K., except for my dreams. My dreams are my biggest problem. They are almost always about finding my dream stud. My dreams have never really worked out. I have been fucked by a lot of hung men, but none of them fit the bill. Most of them were just centered jerks like Carlos and a few were real wimps. My dreams about finding the perfect super hung top, has been more of a nightmare than a dream.

After high school, I spent 3 years in the Marine Corps. Yes, I was looking for a dominate top. You can say what you want about the Marines, but they were good to me. I had no trouble getting my pretty ass plowed on a regular basis while I was in the Marines. Marines like to fuck and a good-looking guy like me, with a nice looking ass, got all the action that he wanted.

Now that I am out of the service, my veteran benefits are helping to pay my way through college. I'm now a sophomore, majoring in business and things are breaking pretty well for me right now.

When I started college, I had decided to stop the stupid dreaming and to get more in touch with reality. I had come to the conclusion that Mr. Perfect, did in fact, not exist and that dreaming about him was just self-destructive. During the last year and a half, my life was centered around my studies and occasionally getting royally fucked by my man Carlos. That is I was at peace with myself, before I saw him.

His name was Mark. The first time I saw him in the main hallway of the Science Building he set off my dominate man alarm like crazy. He was the campus stud, the captain of the college wrestling team and the star quarterback of football team.

He was extremely good-looking, dark haired, college Senior. He stood about 6'2" in height and probably weighed in at about 235 pounds of well-defined muscle. Since he usually wore just a t-shirt and a pair of jeans, I could see that he had board shoulders and a very muscular chest, with large pecs, that tapered down to a slim muscular waist. His arms were, I would say, about 17 inches or more. All of this physical talent was accented by two well-rounded, melon shaped buns that really filled out a pair of jeans, with a very ample bulge in his crotch.

I soon found out from some friends that he was ex-military. He had been a Navy Seal, a fact that really turned me on.

Physically, Mark was not just another college jock he was a college god, but to leave it at that would leave out the parts that really made Mark different and highly attractive to me. Mark had a very adult, experienced demeanor about him. He was the number one college stud, but he didn't really fit into the college jock social scene. His grades were too good, straight A's; his attitude was too adult to fit into the usual college boy social scene. Mark was a young college stud that stood, head and shoulders, above his college counterparts.

All the college young men looked up to him and some, like me, even worshipped him, but he did not act like the typical college jock. He seldom socialized with other college students. Academics and sports were his thing and he never seemed to date, or have a girlfriend, a fact that really interested me to no end.

All of my lusting after Mark might have amounted to nothing, if it wasn't for the fact that I joined the college wrestling team mainly to see what Mark looked like naked. In high school, I was an all-state wrestling champion, but I had no ambition to take up wrestling again until I found out that Mark was the team captain. The first time that I saw him naked in the shower room I was so turned on that I had to turn around and face the shower room wall, like a straight guy taking a shower, in order to keep my dick under control. Mark had a very defined, extremely muscular body. You know the type, the body that looks like it has muscles on top of its muscles. The crown and glory was his big fucking dick. It was thick and over 9 inches long. Yes, he had a great body, but was he gay? My gaydar was ringing off the chart, but I've been wrong in the past. This whole, is he or isn't he thing, made me uptight for months.

There seemed to be no solution to my problem until one night I just happened to luck out. The wrestling team was finishing a practice session in the mat room, when Mark and Gary decided to stay a little longer. Since mark is the team captain, the coach just handed him the keys to the gym and the rest of us just got dressed and started to file out the door.

Mark and Gary were left alone in the mat room. Gary was one of the assistant coaches for the team. He was average looking, with a slim, muscular, semi-hairy body. Mark and Gary had been friends since childhood.

Half way down the block, I realized that I had left my apartment keys in my gym locker. So I hurried back to get them, before Mark locked up the gym.

As I opened my locker, to get my keys, I could hear what sounded like an argument coming from the mat room. I was eager to know what would get a very even-tempered guy like Mark to argue about anything, so I quietly walked up to the second story viewer area, that over looked the mat room. I knew that I stood little chance of being seen, since the lights of the viewer area were shut off.

As I sat down in the back of the dark viewer's area, I could see and hear Mark really telling off Gary. Gary was just sitting on the wrestling mat, as Mark yelled at him, "You asshole, I trusted you all these years and how do you repay me, by stealing from me. If there is anything that I really hate, it's a goddamn thief, especially one who is supposed to be one of my friends." Gary acted scared, "Man I'm sorry, I will find a way to pay you back your $300 bucks." Mark looked unconvinced.

I'm supposed to wait for you to find a way to pay me back! I'm not in the mood to cut you any slack Gary. No, you will start to pay it back, right here and now." Gary looked confused. "How can I do that, I haven't got any money on me?" Mark proceeded to take off his sweatshirt, revealing a very sweat covered, muscular torso. "I've known you for years Gary and I know all your dirty little secrets." Gary got up on his knees and said, "Please, Mark don't, I'll do anything you want, just don't tell on me." Mark looked down at Gary and smiled, "So Gary, you want me to keep quiet, than you will do just as I say and start paying me back, hear and now. You will start by doing just what I already know that you are good at. You're going to help me with my stiff cock problem, aren't you?" Gary did not argue anymore with Mark, he just said, "Yes Sir!" Mark acted pleased at Gary's response he seemed to have some experience in how to play this game.

Mark smiled at Gary and said, "Alright asshole strip, I want you buck naked, get moving asshole!"

"Yes Sir!"

As Gary quickly started to take off his gym clothes, I could see that Mark was starting to get a roaring hard-on. This scene was really turning him on. When Gary was naked, he waited on his knees for his next order. Mark looked half-pleased, as he looked over his naked prize.

"Alright asshole, now take off my shoes and socks."

"Yes Sir!"

As Gary untied Mark's shoe laces and pulled his shoes and socks off, Mark's cock was getting so hard it almost popped out of his gym shorts. At this point, Mark's cock wasn't the only cock that was getting hard. Gary's dick was standing at attention, not to mention mine.

Mark now seemed to be ready for the next act of his pay back drama he quickly slipped off his gym shorts and jock strap, exposing a big, stiff, throbbing hard-on. Gary looked, both a little startled and obviously turned-on, by the sight of Mark's big, stiff cock, throbbing up and down only inches away from his face.

Mark now gave Gary his next order, "Get down on all fours asshole!"

"Yes Sir!"

After Gary was on his hands and knees Mark grabbed the head of his cock, pulled it back towards his waist, then he stepped forward, and put his feet on each of Gary's hands. This put Mark's firm, hairless balls almost right up against Gary's mouth, "All right asshole, start licking my balls!"

"Yes Sir!"

Gary quickly started to massage each of mark's balls, first up one side and then down the other. Mark's body began to mildly shake, as he seemed to be enjoying the Gary's hot, wet tongue playing with his balls.

When Mark was satisfied with Gary's performance, he grabbed Gary by the back of his head and positioned his face for his next job. As Mark held Gray's head back by his hair, he pulled back the head of his big cock, leaned back a little and let go. Mark's big cock slapped against the right side of Gary's face, as Mark started to repeatedly cock slap both sides of Gary's face he said, "Well Gary, you stop play your stupid little victim game, I've known for years that you've been hungry for my cock. You really think that I'm just going to give it to you, like some type of reward, after what you did? No Gary, you're going to have to sincerely beg for it. Gary didn't even stop to think, he just started several minutes of very sincere begging, "Please Sir, may I suck your cock, please Sir –."

Finally, Mark looked down at Gary, pulled back the head of his big cock toward his waist and let go. Mark's cock slapped Gary square in the middle of his face. Mark was really enjoying humiliating Gary, as he knelt, naked in front of him. He then ordered Gary to, "Start licking my cock dog boy, get it wet!"

"Yes Sir!"

"Lick it like a dog, asshole!"

"Yes Sir!"

Gary's head eagerly sprang forward and he started licking Mark's big, throbbing hard cock, from the head, all the way down the shaft. Than Mark ordered Gary to, "Suck my cock you dog and suck it good."

"Yes Sir!"

Gary proceeded to take Mark's cock in his mouth, almost down to the hair, in one fast movement.

After watching Gary deep throat Mark's huge cock several times, all I could think of was this guy's got real talent. At this point, I was getting so turned-on that I unzipped my pants and started to pump my own cock, as I eagerly waited to see what would happen next.

After several minutes of Gary's deep throat cock sucking Mark's breathing started to get heavy and his whole body tensed-up. He began to moan, louder and louder, as his body started to shake as if he was about to shoot a big load of cum down Gary's very hungry throat, when he abruptly pulled his cock out of Gary's mouth and started to stroke it, as he pulled Gary's head back by his hair. Mark moaned loudly and he started to cum. Mark's well-aimed cock, shot stream after stream of sticky cum, all over Gary's face.

After Mark shot his last shot of cum, he backed away. Gary just knelt silently, with his head bowed in front of Mark, cum dripping down his face on to his chest. Mark just stared at Gary in silence for a moment and then he said, "Well asshole, do you think one good blow job will make up for what you did?"

Gary quickly replied, "No Sir!"

Mark started to walk around Gary, "You're right, asshole!" One blowjob won't hack it. You will have to do a lot better than that."

Gary slowly answered, "Please Sir, tell me what I need to do to make things right with you?"

On hearing Gary's reply, Mark started to smile a little.

"Well asshole, I'll tell you what you are going to do to make it right. Now asshole, a weeklong break is coming up in just a few days. You will spend that week at my ranch (Mark was given a ranch by his family trust fund), as my personal slave. You will do anything that I order you to do. You will clean my house, do chores around the ranch, fix my meals and service my cock. Asshole, before you are even with me you are going to know what it's like to be completely owned by a man and what it's like to exist only to please your master.

Mark started to walk around Gary again, his still rock hard cock pulsating up and down, inspecting his naked captive and waiting for a reaction to what he just said, Gary just sat silently on the mat, cum still dripping off of his face. Mark stopped in front of Gary and said, "Well asshole, do you have any problems with what you are going to do during the break.

Gary almost shouted his reply, "No Sir! It will be my pleasure to serve you in any way that I can, Sir!"

Gary's reply seemed to please Mark, as he smiled and he then walked over to his backpack and pulled out a towel. After throwing the towel at Gary, Mark said. "O.K. asshole, clean yourself up, I won't have my slave looking bad. Now take your slave ass home and don't forget where you belong at 8:00 A.M. this Saturday, asshole!"

"Yes Sir! It will be an honor to serve you Sir!"

As Gary and Mark started to get dressed, I made a silent and fast exit from the gym. All the way home I had a roaring hard-on, while I said to myself, over and over again, "Damn, why does Gary have to be so lucky, why does –." That night I had a lot of trouble getting any sleep.

There was only two school days left before the big holiday break and only one more training session for the college wrestling team. As I walked through the gym door to practice with the team, Mark greeted me, "Hi Randy, good to see you again."

Mark's greeting and demeanor startled me a little. He was more friendly than normal and his eyes seemed to look right through me. All of which made me a little nervous.

After the practice session, the coach gave me the task of cleaning up and locking up the gym. When everyone was gone and I was finished putting the equipment away, I couldn't help but go over what had happened in the gym, between Mark and Gary. The idea of being Gary, kneeling naked in front of Mark's big, hard, throbbing cock, started to make my dick hard. I went over to the area of the gym where Mark had stood and I started to go over the events of the night in my mind. All of a sudden, I noticed something that startled me. I looked up at the viewer's area from the spot where Mark had stood getting his big cock sucked and I saw something that I had never noticed about the viewer's area.

At the far, right hand corner was a big round security mirror. Ahhh Shit! He could see me up there. The big stud knew that I was up there the whole time!"

All the way home, I tried to figure out what to do about the fact that Mark knew that I was watching him and Gary. Did this mean that I was in trouble, or what? On the other hand, was this some type of opportunity for me to do a Gary type of act with Mark? After all, I have a much better looking body than Gary and Mark keeps giving me that hungry animal look, like I'm fresh meat, or something. What should I do?

When the holiday break was over I still didn't know what to do about my Mark problem. While I was walking down the hallway of the Social Science Building I ran into a solution to my problem, my old high school friend Mike.

"Hi Randy, I hope that you will help your class out, just like last year. We're going to do the same thing again. Hell! With your good looks and my big dick (It is 12 inches long) we can raise a lot of money. Here hand these out."

Mike gave me a pile of fliers that announced the Sophomore Class Slave Auction. I was in it last year. Some girl had bought me to do her homework and wash her car. God! It was boring!"

After thinking about it a little, I started to smile. Yes why not, it may work.

That day I saw Mark in the Science Building and I asked to talk to him in private. I handed him a flier and then said, "I hope you will help me and my class. I'm going to be one of the slaves being sold. If you buy me I will do anything that you want."

At this moment Mark's eyes lit up as he stared into my eyes.

"What do you mean by anything, Randy?"

This was the moment of truth, would I have the nerve?

"I will keep care of your property, fix your meals and exercise your cock any way that you want me to (I can't believe I just said that). The last part is just between you and me."

Mark smiled, "I'll have to think about it."

He then smiled and slapped me on the back and said, "Later." Mark than started to walk down the hall as I watched his him disappear into the crowd I felt the tension leave my body. Well, I took a shoot. Did I score? I just had to wait and see.

The auction had a good turnout, about one hundred students. I wore a tight pair of jeans and a tank top in order to show off my good points. The slaves were to be sold for one day of labor. When it was my turn to be sold, I looked around the room, but I saw no sign of Mark, my heart sank. Did I make a big mistake? The opening bid on me was $10 and the bids slowly climbed to $40 and stalled. I looked around the room one more time, still no Mark. Well, it seems my plan is a bust and the pretty blond guy is going to be sold to a homely girl again. My heart sank and I just bowed my head and looked at the floor. Well, at least I still have my man Carlos.

At dawn the next morning, I started the new day the way, that up to now, I had only dreamed about, on my back, with a big dick up my ass. As I placed my feet on my man's shoulders he started to slowly fuck me, until my ass finally accepted every inch of his mammoth meat.

I moaned louder and louder as my body started to violently squirm as my man started to really shove it to me. As the minutes passed the sexual tension in my body started to become unbearable. My cock was now so hard it was starting to hurt. Just as I was close to cumming I lifted my upper body off the mattress and grabbed hold of my man's shoulders, as he leaned over me, forcing the trusts of his huge cock to repeatedly massage my prostate gland and send me over the edge.

Just as my man started to shoot his load up my hungry ass my whole body tensed up and I let out a loud scream, just as my cock erupted, shooting stream after stream of warm, sticky cum all over my upper body. When my cock was spent my whole body started to relax and I put my feet down on the mattress as my man withdrew his still hard cock from my ass. He then leaned forward and gave me a long, slow kiss as beads of sweat dripped off his body on to mine.

As he withdrew his lips from mine, he sat up, started to run his hands over my folded legs a few times, and said, "Man I bought myself a really great fuck last night."

As I smiled, he then grabbed one of my knees and flipped me over on my stomach as he slapped my bare ass several times.

"Now, for the rest of the day I own your ass. Get up slave and clean yourself up. We are leaving for my ranch. I intend to get a lot of work out of you today, before I fuck that great ass of yours again. Also, if I am pleased with you today you can spend the night with me."

"Yes Sir! Anything you say."

Looking at Mark's naked backside as he walked into the bathroom was a sight that I had only been able to dream about for the last several months. But, he was really here, I was not dreaming. I could only think, "Man, it does not get any better than this.

Mark had waited for the very last moment before buying me at the auction. It seemed he is a real drama queen. Now he owns me for a whole day and I intend to give him more than his money's worth. Then maybe, just maybe, he will want to keep me. Well, I can dream can't I?

CHAPTER SIX

MEMORIES

God, talk about being horny. When I started to get undressed to take a shower my fat, dependable, nine-inch cock, quickly sprang to attention. My big dick was so hard it almost hurt. I had not allowed myself to cum in almost a month and the sexual tension in my body had reached a new peak. I had to get off, or I would probably have an accident, like shooting a load in my pants, or having a wet dream.

Just after I stepped into the shower and the warm spray started to soak my tense body, I reached for a bottle of lubricant. I applied a generous amount to my throbbing cock and I slowly started to stroke.

Several times I had to stop and let my cock throb up and down freely, while I tried to think about unrelated things, anything that would keep me from cumming to fast. But, I must admit that I love the feeling of my body teasing up as I get close to cumming. I've really gotten addicted to that huge surge of muscle tensing, erotic energy that you get just before shooting a big load. But, after about 10 minutes the pump was way over primed and I could not stop. With warm water running down my back I pointed my stiff cock upward, I took a few fast strokes, my body tensed up and I shoot off a big load that spattered against the shower stall ceiling. It was soon followed by several more bursts, only two of which actually hit the ceiling the rest fell short of the mark.

Done with releasing a month's worth of erotic tension, I suddenly felt a little weak. I grabbed both sides of the shower to keep my balance. My little cock-shooting contest had really drained a lot of energy out of me and I momentarily felt a little faint. After a few minutes of deep breathing I quickly recovered my strength. I than slowly soaped up, my still sensitive naked body and then quickly rinsed off.

After toweling off I headed for my bedroom to get a brief rest lying face down naked on my bed. As my body relaxed I mentally relieved the erotic moment that I had just experienced. Man, what a rush that was!

You know, if you work it right, a simple sexual act like masturbation can be developed into a major event in your life rather than just a another way to get your rocks off. I'm like any other horny, young, gay guy, I need a method to relieve my pent up sexual energy, or I will simply go nuts. I'm a firm believer in the old phrase, "Use it or lose it." But, I am not a guy that beats off several times a day, even when I feel like it. I am different from my horny friends in one very distinct way, I want the act of having sex to be something to remember, not just a routine, or daily event.

I guess that I can blame my feelings about sex partly on my Grandmother. She always kept telling me that, "The only events in your life that you will remember when you are old are the really good and the really bad moments in your life. So, prepare for and try to have as many really good moments as possible and if possible record the event on film. My grandmother was big fan of scrapbooks and photo albums.

So, I have tried to follow my grandmother's advice in business, sports, academics, in fact any activity that is a major part of my life. I think my grandmother would approve of my way of doing things, but I don't think that she would have ever thought that I would apply her wisdom to sex acts, but that is what has happened.

Because of the way that I live my life, especially my gay sex life, most gay guys think that I am a little snobby, strange or anti-social. But, since I am a 28-year-old gay male, with a 6'2", 225 pound, muscular, gym toned body people tend to overlook such human flaws.

People tell me that I am very good-looking. I am what other gay guys call a very hot number. This fact should have given me a big edge in getting laid, but sometimes pluses can become minuses. Because I am not available much, quite a few local gay guys don't seem to like me. I have developed an image problem. This image problem can at times stand in the way of any plans I may have.

When I get one of my strange sexual urges I try to find the type of person that fits into my fantasy. If I find what I am looking for I like to get to know him personally and do some research to find out if a potential sex partner is right for me and not just a way to put another notch on my big cock. To me quality is much more important than quantity. With such encounters, I usually try to snap some photos for my album, or shoot some film. Even high quality tricks can just walk through your life, but photos are forever.

I call my collection of photos my memories book. My friends call it a trick book. People see things differently.

When I have sex with someone I like to do something different, with a hot number that I have taken the time to get to know. I also, talk to people who have had sex with them to find out if they up to the challenge, so to speak. No, I don't want to just have sex, get my rocks off etc. I want a brand new experience and possibly even set a personal best type of record. I want to do something, like my shower stall, hit the ceiling scene. Such a sexual outlet will satisfy my sexual needs and possibly give me a real head-trip too. But, it can be frustrating at times. Like in the case of my last try, up till now I have been unable to hit the ceiling more than three times in one session. It was a real rush, but not a personal record.

When I get an idea about doing something different with some brand new, hot number, I will go out to places that I know hot gay guys will hang out and start my search. I know the type of sex partner that will satisfy my needs. I have a clear picture of how he looks, his body, how big his cock is, how much body hair he will have, color of hair etc. After I find one or several young men that fit the bill I will start the process of getting to know them and finding out what they like to do and are good at. Some of the information comes from the person himself, but most of the time it comes from friends who have had sex with him. The whole process can takes up to several months.

The whole process can be really frustrating, but when it works well, it really works well. A good example of this principal is Chuck. I got this idea in my head that I wanted to fuck a really hot, smooth bodied, blond guy all night long. So naturally, I needed to find a number that turns me on that really loves to be fucked for hours at a time. Even among chronic bottom men this is a rare number.

I found Chuck at a popular gay bathhouse. Friends had told me about him and his abilities. Since he physically fit the type that I was looking for, I decided to show up at the baths the one night a friend said that he would be there.

Chuck fit the bill and I got lucky, we hit it off right away. I fucked him off and on for at least 6 hours. We both shot our loads five times. That was a night neither of us will soon forget. Chuck is now a three times a year scene with me and I have some great naked photos of him and me in my album.

No matter how much I plan or what strange urges I may get, some situations just sort of fall into my lap. These are scenes that I never would have gone out to look for. The odds of finding such sexual situations are much more chance than planning.

I ran into just such a wild scene six months ago and I still smile whenever I think about them. Who are them? They are stuff of gay and straight men's fantasies – twins. Not just any run of the mill twins, but good-looking, hot, sexy twins.

Their names were Steve and Randy Johnston. I had met them briefly over a year ago at a party for a close friend and then they were gone. It seems that I got in on the tail end of their yearly summer visit to L.A., that is the last few minutes before they had to run to catch a plane to fly to Boston. It was one of those, their eyes lit up, they smiled, you were introduced and they were gone, brief scenes. It may have been short and sweet, but it left a deep impression on my mind.

This last summer I run into them by accident at a local gay restaurant. I was in luck, they were with a friend of mine and he introduced us again. Well, over the next five days, one thing led to another and I invited them to my house lunch and a swim in my pool.

Since, I really didn't know how to handle a three-way sex scene I was a little nervous. But, I need not have worried. After Steve and Randy arrived it soon became apparent that they had lots of experience in such situations.

I finished giving them a brief tour of my home with a stop in my bedroom. Both of them seemed to be fascinated by the big sky light over my king sized bed. The whole room was bathed in sun light. I than asked them if they wanted something to eat or drink. They spoke almost at the same time, "Yes, we would like something special to eat."

With that statement they both walked over to me and whispered in the ears. "We want you for lunch, stud."

Their clothes and mine were soon piled on the floor and as they started to approach me I quickly inspected their naked bodies. They were both about 5'10" tall, with very healthy looking, flawless, smooth skin. Their cocks were about eight inches long and rapidly throbbing up and down. They were both really turned-on. They started kissing my neck as I started to fondle the two of them.

Now, Steve said, "Just stand still stud, we will handle everything."

With that statement they both gave me a deep kiss before they dropped down on their knees and started to lick, message and kiss my feet. God that felt soooon good as my cock sprang to attention. A fact not lost on the twins as they both reached up and began to gently tickle my balls as they continued to give my feet a warm bath. My body started to mildly shake.

Within a minute both of them were licking my balls as their finger caressed my legs and the crack of my ass. Just after licked the length of my throbbing hard cock several times, one of them deep throated my big cock while the other stood up and started to tongue and mildly bite my nipples. The dual erotic sensation of someone giving me a fantastic blowjob and some else playing with my nipples was starting to drive me crazy.

I grabbed both of the twins by the hair on the back of their heads, lifting one to his feet, and in turn I started to make out with the both of them, as my hands caressed their backs and the crack of their asses. They both started to moan. They really liked the light touch of a man's hands.

Now, I dropped to my knees and one after the other, again and again, I sucked each of their cocks, clear down to the hair. Just as it seemed that each of them was getting really turned-on, they both grabbed one of my shoulders and pulled me to my feet. As they started to make out with me again they both reached under my arms and pushed upward, forcing my arms up over my head. I held my hands together as both the twins lick their way down my neck, until their tongues were playing with my nipples. Next, they moved over and began to lick my armpits, from one end to the other, again and again, as their hands mildly caressed the sides of my torso. This neat little trick soon had me moaning and shaking big time. In just a few minutes I had to stop them. They kissed me once more, smiled like they had something naughty on their minds, before they gently shoved me down on to the bed.

As one of them kneeled down and put his cock in my mouth the other greased up my throbbing, hard dick. Soon I was slowly sucking one of the twin's cocks as I felt the warm sensation of my cock sliding deep into the other twin's ass. As one twin rode my cock the other fucked my mouth.

In only a few minutes it appeared to breathe faster. Suddenly, the twin fucking my mouth started to moan and squirm, his cock swelled just before he unloaded down my throat. As I swallowed a load of warm, sweet cum, my body violently shook and my cock exploded into the other twin's ass, just as I heard a loud moan before I started to feel warm cum splatter on my chest.

After cleaning up in the bathroom we rested for a while on my bed with the bright summer sun warming our naked bodies. With one twin on each side of me I started to daydream about what would come next. I was hoping that after having something to eat and maybe a swim in the pool it would be time for round two of my twin's fantasy, the round in which I get to royally fuck both of the twins, one after the other. I looked up at the ceiling and smiled. Man, this was sure a wild scene and I have it on film too. You see my room has cameras in all four walls and two in the ceiling. Yes, I am going to remember this day for a long, long time.

CHAPTER SEVEN

FANTASY LOVER

PUBLISHED IN TORSO MAGAZINE: JUNE 2006

Man, it was a real rush, helping to run the hologram booth at "Galaxy" for the New Year's party. My friend Paul and I had decided to program all of the hologram images of naked, famous gay porn stars to all cum at 12:00 P.M. and usher in the new year of 2040. At the stroke of 12 all the life like porn star images on the stage and dance platforms shot their loads right on time and the audience seemed to really dig it. I got a real feeling of accomplishment, a natural high so to speak, that is until my lover showed up.

My lover Greg came into the booth, taped me on the shoulder and said, "Let's go James, I've had enough of this New Year's shit, I'm going home." That his usual down beat way of telling me that we were leaving. He has always been a sooooo in charge type of personality, which is a fact that I have never liked about him. In the three years that I have lived with him I have not been able to change any of his personality problems one bite. He is very self-centered, uncaring and he can be a real snob.

Why has a drop dead gorgeous, young blond guy like me stayed with such a jerk? Well, it is the typical L.A. young, hung and pretty, gay guy story, he is rich, decent looking and he has a big dick. But, after three years of mental torture I have decided that I have had enough. My New Year's resolution this year is to dump the jerk and to find a decent lover, no matter how long it takes.

Maybe, I have matured as a person. I no longer believe that the use of a new BMW, charge cards and living in a Beverly Hills mansion is all that important. Such things have lost their attraction to me. I have begun to see that my friend Paul is right; personal relationships are what really matter in life. I have lots of material things, but when it comes to personal relationships, except for Paul, I am living in a slum and starving to death.

The next morning, while my lover was away playing golf with his rich buddies again, I packed up my stuff, wrote my lover a "Dear John" type of letter, left the BMW keys, the charge cards and my house keys on the dining room table and I left to move in with a friend of mine.

About a week after I made my break from my boring lover I ran into my friend Paul at a popular bar in the new "Boys Town" area of West Hollywood. He acted excited to see me as he smiled and started up a conversation in a fairly quiet corner of the bar. "Well James, I hear that you finally dumped your jerk of a lover, are you ready for a Forget Your Ex-Lover type of vacation?" I didn't know what to really say. "A what?"

"I have a new business that I just opened. It is a high-tech fantasy vacation business."

"Wow, you own one of those fall asleep and dream a vacation businesses. I have heard of them, but I don't know much about them." Paul smiled and then handed me a small booklet. "Here, this will explain everything. Since you are my best friend you can have your first vacation free. It will be my way of helping you to get over the lousy relationship that you just got rid of."

The idea was worth considering I put the booklet in my back pocket and thanked Paul. As Paul started to work the crowd handing out his new business information I decided to walk over to popular gay restaurant and get a bite to eat.

The restaurant was packed, but I managed to get a small two-person table and just after ordering a drink and a light meal I noticed him. He was a dark haired, good-looking, young man, who was sitting on the other side of the bar. I could see by the tight shirt that he was wearing that he had a very muscular and well defined body. He kept staring at me and smiling. His attention did not make me even a little up-tight, it started to feel good.

After finishing my meal I got up and went to the bathroom. He followed me. As I washed my hands he just stood behind me, leaning against the wall with a big smile on his face. I noticed that he was developing a big bulge in his pants, indicating that he was nicely equipped. Suddenly, he said, "I wonder; are you going to be a good date, or just another big disappointment in my life?" I was so nervous that I didn't know what to say.

Well, his name was Vince and I went on the date and I spent the night with him. To say that the sex was great would have been an understatement. But, it did not stop with just that night. The next morning I awoke lying on my back with a warm, wet, erotic feeling in my crotch. I lifted my head up to see that the covers on the bed had been dumped on the floor and Vince was between my legs slowly sucking my cock as his fingers caressed my firm balls. The feeling was incredible. "God, that feeeels sooo good."

I was still so horny that it only took a few minutes of Vince's talented cock sucking to get me close to climax. My body started to squirm, jerk and get rigid. I gritted my teeth and grabbed the mattress cover with both of my hands, just as my cock unloaded in Vince's warm, wet mouth.

As I shot my load the sensation of Vince's tongue licking the head of my cock as he rapidly stroked my cock and tickled my balls started to drive me crazy. My body violently shook and I almost screamed. Finally, I could not take it any longer I lifted my upper body off the mattress and grabbed my cock. "Pleasseee stop you're driving me crazzzy."

Vince stopped and sat up and smiled, cum was dripping down his chin. He then leaned forward and licked his way up my stomach and chest and then he gave me a long, slow, wet kiss before he backed off and said, "How was that for a wakeup call, Babe?"

Vince was not through with me. He now told me to turn over. I soon felt his hands lightly caress the muscles of my back. As I lifted my head off the pillow and turned to face Vince he smiled and said, "Well Babe, your body feels a little tense and I'm going to loosen you up a little. I just put my head back down on the mattress as Vince instructed me to put my arms at my side and to relax.

I did just as I was told. Vince quickly mounted me and sat down on my bare ass, with his big cock touching the lower part of my back. A spark of sexual tension flashed threw my barely awake body and my cock started to get hard again. I now felt Vince's hands start to firmly massage my upper body, starting with my neck and working his way down my back and back up again.

After about 20 minutes of deep tissue massaging my neck, shoulders and back, Vince lifted off of my body and stood on the side of the bed, as he started to work on my right leg, his now rock hard cock repeatedly throbbed up and down. When he got to my feet he started to work on pressure points. Each time that he really dug into a point my body tensed up and I started to moan. "Oh good, Ahhh!"

After about another half hour of one of the most relaxing massage that I have ever had Vince was done. He then slapped my bare ass really hard. "O.K. Babe get up, it's time for a shower."

When I was up and standing next to the bed Vince noticed that I had a big, throbbing hard hard-on. He smiled, than grabbed me by my hard dick and led me into the bathroom.

After I had finished shaving off the few whiskers that I have on my boyish face I took a quick shower, dried off and then walked into the bedroom and started to do some exercises to limber up a little more. When Vince walked into the bedroom I was doing pushups with my nearly soft cock rubbing the carpet each time that I lowered my body almost to the floor.

"Well Babe, are you in the mood to show you a more interesting way to do pushups." Without waiting for a reply he told me to spread my legs far apart while he got down on his knees between my legs. He quickly ran his arms under my upper legs. He then lifted my lower body off the ground. "O.K. Babe, now put your legs on my shoulders and continue doing your push-ups." As I started to lower my upper body again, Vince's hands parted my ass cheeks and I soon felt a warm, wet tongue start to lick my asshole. My whole body just shook and I started to moan. "Ahhhh..."

For the next ten minutes or so I enjoyed and fought the duel sensations of having my ass expertly rimmed as the pain in my arms and shoulders starting too built up as I did as many push-ups as I could. My cock started to throb harder and harder as I got close to climax. Finally, I could not take it anymore and I just collapsed on my face just as I shot my load on the bedroom carpet, while Vince continued to rim my ass as my body violently squirmed.

When it was all over I just laid on the carpet for a moment breathing hard. When my breathing had returned to normal I quickly got up on my knees only to come face to face with Vince's throbbing hard, 8-inch cock. I looked up at his smiling face our little game was not over yet. I knew an invitation when I see one staring me in the face.

I buried my face in Vince's crotch and started to eagerly lick his big, firm, hairless balls. The scent and taste of his crotch started to drive my already hard cock wild. I was still so horny that I spent several minutes just bathing Vince's balls in warm saliva as my rock hard cock just throbbed up and down. Vince's body squirmed and he started to moan. "Damn you're good at that." As I proceeded to tongue his big cock, from its hairy base to its plump head, his cock started to pulsate up and down, as if it was playing a game with my tongue.

When I swallowed his cock almost down to its base Vince started to rapidly moan and his body tensed up. As I continued to deep throat his rock hard cock his moaning grew louder. Just as I moved my hands down to massage the side of his legs and feet, Vince's cock started to firm up as his body violently shook. "Oh Good, I'm going to cum." I now felt Vince grab the back of my head with both of his hands as he shoved his big cock down my throat just as he started to unload a big load of sweet, warm cum down my eager throat.

After Vince's cock started to soften I licked his cock clean and then stood up. He placed his hands under my armpits and lifted me to my feet. He then started to give me a long, deep kiss, as his hands lightly massaged the length of my back until his fingers were caressing the crack of my ass. I started to moan and shake. He continued to kiss my lips, face, neck and shoulders and give my back and ass a gentle finger massage for several minutes. I moaned and my body shook. After he had finished with me he backed off, looked deep into my eyes, and smiled, "Well Babe, it seems we need to take another shower."

As I watched Vince walk naked into the bathroom I just sat on the edge of the bed sort of counting my blessings. Jesus, he is one beautiful hunk of a man. I hope that he is a keeper. Than it happened!

Suddenly, several bright lights went on. I couldn't see anything for a moment. When my eyes started to clear up I could make out a familiar figure, it was Paul. "Well James, how was your fantasy vacation?" Reality was finely setting in, "Oh Shit, it was just a fantasy. Vince and the whole date was just a dream, one of my friend Paul's Hi-Tech Fantasy Vacations. My perfect man was not real.

After I cleaned up, I had a chance to talk to Paul in his office. I had some questions that I needed to get answers too. "Paul where did you get a program like that, it was fantastic?"

"I wrote and designed the whole thing."

"Really, how did you come up with a character like Vince and a plot like that?" Paul smiled for a moment. "I didn't make it up really. I patterned Vince after me and your part was patterned after my late lover Brad." (Paul's lover had been killed in a car accident about a year ago.) Now, it started to make more sense. If you take away Vince's face you would be left with Paul's body.

Paul and I had been roommates and fuck buddies in college, but I did not mentally make the connection, I was just too wrapped up in the fantasy.

"Wow, you mean sex with your lover was that great?"

Paul half smiled as if he was remembering a fond memory.

"Yes, I really miss Brad. We were great together. He was not only my lover he was my best friend too."

Then it hit me, had I really been that dumb all these years. I had not seen what was right in front of my own eyes. I just had to ask Paul, "Paul do you think best friends like us would make good lovers?" Paul looked directly at me and smiled and his eyes just lit up. He didn't have to say a thing I had my answer.

CHAPTER EIGHT

PORN INTERVIEW

PUBLISHED IN MANDATE MAGAZINE: JULY 2005

When the alarm went off, the sun was just starting to light up my bedroom. I quickly rolled out from under the covers and sat naked on the side of my bed. The cold morning air made my already hard cock throb.

After getting up, I walked over to the closet. My hard cock bounced up and down, making me even more horny. As I opened the closet door to get a pair of jeans to wear, I noticed the reflection of my nude body in the full-length mirror on the inside of the closet door. I had never really looked at myself before. The image standing before me was of a naked, smooth bodied, hung, 19 year old, pretty blond, young male, with a throbbing hard-on. I had a good-looking, semi-muscular, swimmer's body, with only a little public hair. I quickly turned around and ran my hands over my nicely rounded, hairless butt. Today, this naked young man in the mirror was going to have to find a solution to a big problem in his life.

The problem was that I was deeply in debt. My visa card was maxed out, I had no saving and my car needed work. Being a retail queen just was not paying the bills. I had to get a new source of income.

That is why my friend Hank offered to get me a job in the porn industry. The idea made me a little nervous at first, but Hank worked hard to convince me.

"Hell, Jimmy you are a chicken hawks wet dream. You have one hell of a sexy body. I can get you an interview with a major company. Just say the word."

"O.K. Hank, you can get me an interview, but what do I say and do to get hired?"

"Look Jimmy, you already have the body and the outgoing personality. Just remember, when the guy interviews you just figure out what he wants, than give him more than he expected. Also, try to be creative in what you say and do, its porn, but it is still show business."

The interview was at a house in the Hollywood Hills. I parked my car about half a block away and just sat still for a moment. I was a little nervous and I needed a few minutes to get myself together. I didn't know what to expect. I had heard some bad things about porn companies; was I doing the right thing? As I got out of my car I repeated over and over again in my head, figure want he wants, give him more than he expects, be creative.

The house was a one-story Spanish style home with a red tile porch. As I walked to the front door and rang the bell, I could see through the side glass panels that the house had a pool in the back yard, surrounded by a beautiful garden. The house took my breath away they don't have houses like this in rural Ohio, where I grew up, not even close.

A good-looking young man opened the door. I recognized him right away. He was Chuck Wade a major porn star. He looked me over from head to toe and smiled. I now felt more relaxed. Well, at least he wasn't the fat old troll that I had expected to meet.

He offered me his hand. "Hi, I'm Chuck and you must be Jimmy."

I shook his hand and smiled. Maybe, this was going to be a good experience. Chuck opened the front door and motioned for me to follow him into the house.

"Just put your stuff on the sofa in the living room and get naked."

Chuck than disappeared into the kitchen. I didn't even stop to think why he wanted to start our interview with me in the nude, I only knew that this Chuck fellow was starting to ready turn me on and showing him my naked body seemed like a great way to get him interested. After all no one had ever told me that I had a bad looking body.

When Chuck returned he had two glasses of wine in his hands. He stopped for a brief moment and he just stared wide eyed at me. I smiled; it seemed Chuck definitely liked what he saw. Chuck gave me one of the glasses of wine as his eyes inspected my naked body. Without saying a word he walked around me, looking me over, as I took a few sips of wine.

"God damn, Hank was telling me the truth you really do have a great looking body and one hell of a big dick. Just looking at you has me so turned on I feel like picking you up and taking you to my bed and making love to every inch of you and that's just for starters."

I knew that this was the opening that I wanted and I put down my glass of wine on the coffee table and walked over to stand in front of Chuck. As my stiff, throbbing cock bounced off the front of his jeans, I stared into his beautiful eyes, put my arms around his shoulders and gave him a slow, deep kiss, as I felt his hands move down my back and grasp my bare ass.

When I withdrew my lips from his he firmly grabbed both my ass cheeks, lifted me off the floor and said, "Well Jimmy, do you want to find out how we ball in L.A.?"

I just smiled, "Any time that you are ready."

Chuck did not say a word, he just put one arm around my shoulders, bent over and cupped the back of my legs with the other and lifted me up off the floor. The feel of this powerful, handsome, young man picking me up had my big cock throbbing like crazy. I didn't care about what made sense any more I just knew that I wanted this hot stud.

After Chuck carried me into his bedroom, he put me down in an overstuffed chair, just before he walked over to a sound system and put a tape into the machine. He then turned to face me, "Well sweet cheeks you gave me a nice little show in the living room, now it's my turn."

With that he hit the play button. As the tape began to play he started to do a slow strip tease act. I did not say a word I just sat there watching Chuck slowly take off each piece of his clothing as my big cock throbbed up and down on my stomach.

Chuck's little strip as lasted about 15 minutes as I just sat there wide-eyed, with my mouth slightly open, as his shirt came off, revealing a very muscular and well-defined torso that was well accented by two very developed arms. Next Chuck kicked off his shoes and pulled off his socks, before he started to play a little game with his pants and underwear. He slowly unzipped his pants and let them drop to the floor, before he began to play a slow cock teasing game with his jockey shorts.

Finally, Chuck took his underwear off, revealing a half-hard 8 inch cock, very muscular legs and a nice firm rounded ass. As Chuck started to run his hands over his naked body I was starting to breathe harder. I was so turned on that I felt like shooting my load all over my chest and stomach, right then and there.

At this point I knew that I just had to have him and as the music was ending I got up, walked over to Chuck, got down on my knees, and begged him for his cock.

"Please Sir, may I suck your cock?"

Chuck didn't answer, the music stopped and he bent over and ran his hands over my back down to my ass and back up again. My mouth just watered as his pulsating cock landed right in my face.

"Well, so you want to play."

Chuck now stood up and grabbed his hard cock, exposing his firm, hairless balls and said, "Well sweet cheeks let's see you earn my cock. Start by licking my balls."

"Yes Sir!"

I didn't need any more encouragement I leaned forward and with my warm, moist tongue I started to gently massage his balls. As I licked his balls from one side to the other Chuck began to mildly moan and his legs began to shake. His reaction to my tongue bath only encouraged me to lick faster, as his moaning and shaking grew more intense.

The scent of his crotch and his approving moans had my cock throbbing so wildly that I felt like a dog in heat and I hadn't even got to suck dick yet.

Just as I thought that I was about to get to suck Chuck's cock, I felt a hand grab the back of my head as I heard Chuck say, "Get up, it time for some pec work."

After I stood up my head was pushed on to Chuck's chest and I was told to get to work. I eagerly started to lick Chuck's right nipple as he played with my cock and balls. After only a few minutes of licking his nipples, Chuck raised his right arm and he forced my head over to work on his pit. I licked around the sides of his armpit and then I ran my tongue thought the center several times. Chuck moaned loudly, which only encouraged me. By the time I was licking his other pit I was starting to breathe harder. I was getting close to cumming.

Suddenly, Chuck pulled me off his chest, just as he grabbed the head of my cock and squeezed it really hard. I just stood there, face to face with Chuck, until my cock settled down. Chuck than let go of my cock and gave me a long slow kiss before he put me back to work licking his nipples and pits.

After Chuck seemed very satisfied with my performance I was told to get on my knees. The thought that I was finally going to get Chuck's dick had my cock going wild and I started to breathe faster again. The whole idea of getting to suck this good-looking, porn stud's big cock and maybe even taste his warm, sweet cum, was starting to do a trip on my head.

As I got to my knees, Chuck put his hands on the sides of my head, so that I could not move. He then positioned his cock on my nose and forehead and his balls on my lips.

"Now Boy, I want you to lick one side of my cock and then the other, than you can deep throat my cock, one stroke after another, until I shot a big load down your throat. Do you understand?"

I just moved my head up and down, rubbing his cock and balls in my face. When Chuck backed away from me I quickly started to lick his cock, until it was completely wet. As I slowly swallowed his big cock, clean down to his hair, he let out a loud moan and his whole body shook a little. As I continued to deep throat his cock his moans grew louder. The more that he moaned and his body shook the more tuned on I became.

His reactions to my little performance only encourage me to suck faster as he started to build to climax. Just before he came he let out a loud moan, as he grabbed the back of my head and forced his cock down my throat. He moaned loudly one more time as his cock swelled and he started to pump a big loud of warm, sweet cum down my eager throat. I gagged a little at first, by my throat quickly adjusted as I drank the steady stream of man cum, right down to the last drop.

After Chuck had shot his load I cleaned off the last drops of cum from his still throbbing hard cock with my tongue. I had not had any man sex in over a month and sucking off Chuck had been just like having the best tasting dessert that I've ever had. I only wish that I could have sucked him off 10 more times in a row.

Chuck wasn't going to let me suck him off again he had other plans for his cock. Chuck bent over, put his arms around me, and gave me a long slow kiss.

After several minutes of deep, warm kisses, Chuck stopped and put his hands under my armpits as he gently lifted me to my feet. Chuck looked into my eyes as his hands grabbed my ass cheeks.

"Jimmy you have proven to be such a turn-on that I just have to fuck you."

I just smiled. Chuck smiled too, just before he walked over to the bed and threw back the covers and then he placed two pillows on top of each other in the center of the bed. I don't need to be told what to do I just got on the bed face down with the pillows under my hips.

As my body started to relax I felt Chuck's hands run up and down my naked body, just before I felt a hand slap my bare ass really hard. My body reacted to the blow by tensing up for a few seconds before I relaxed again and I started to eagerly wait for the feel of a Chuck's greased man cock sliding up my ass.

As I waited, I watched Chuck walk over to a desk and get out a jar and several towels. The sight of Chuck's beautiful, well-built naked backside turned on me so bad that I started to move my hips up and down as I dry fucked the pillows.

When Chuck returned I quickly felt several fingers start to play with the crack of my ass. The slow massaging nature of Chuck's fingers soon had my body mildly shaking. Then suddenly, I felt two hands part my ass cheeks and I felt a warm, wet tongue touch my asshole. I tensed up and the front part of my body lifted off the bed. It soon felt so good that I started to moan and my legs shook.

After only a few minutes of what I would call expert rimming, Chuck stopped and my body completely relaxed, just before I felt a hard, greased cock slid deep into my ass in one fast stroke. The force of the thrust of Chuck's cock caused my upper body to lift off the mattress and I let out a loud moan. The next few thrusts were slow and deep, as my ass quickly adjusted to the feel of a man's cock inside of me. I started to moan and squirm as the pleasure of being fucked by a stud man started to really turn me on. Soon, Chuck put his hands on my shoulders and he really started to shove it to me, long and deep. This new position had me moaning and squirming in no time. Just as I was showing signs of getting close to climax Chuck backed off and my body started to relax. It seems that Chuck understood my body as well as I, and he didn't want me to cum just yet.

When my body stopped shacking and I was breathing at a more normal rate, Chuck turned me over on my back, put my legs on his shoulders as he started to really shove it to me again. It only took a few minutes to get me squirming and moaning again as I got close to cumming. But, this time was different, Chuck stopped fucking me for a minute and with a slight smile on his face he said, "Now Jimmy, I want to see you cum without touching yourself. I am going to turn you on and then I will push you over the edge."

It only took Chuck a few minutes of hard fucking to have me moaning and squirming and close to climax, when he started to lick the bottoms and sides of my feet while he lightly caressed my legs. I started to scream and violently squirm. I couldn't hold it back anymore, my cock just erupted and I shot a big load all over myself. When my cock finished unloading, Chuck pulled his cock out of me, yanked the rubber off and just let his cock freely shoot a steady stream of warm, sticky cum all over my chest and stomach.

Chuck now bent over, kissed me, and smiled. He seemed very pleased. "Jimmy you are the best fuck that I have had in a long time. You are really something."

With that he grabbed several towels and he cleaned up the both of us before he pulled me off the bed and said, "O.K. sweet cheeks, let's take a shower."

After the shower we went shinny dipping in the backyard pool. It felt good to swim naked in a heated pool and make out with Chuck again. When we finished our little swim we went back into the bedroom to rest. As Chuck lay down next to me I turned over on my side and put my arms around him with my head on his chest. He put one arm across my back, with his hand on my ass and said, "O.K. now let's get a little sleep." I don't need any more encouragement as I relaxed and we both drifted off to sleep.

Sleeping in the nude with Chuck for a few hours was the most comfortable feeling that I have had in years. The warmth of his muscular body and the soft sound of his beating heart made me feel very content and for the first time in years I felt protected and safe. Being new in L.A. and coming from a small town, I didn't know much about life, especially in the big city, I only knew that I liked this feeling and I wanted it to continue.

I was awakened a few hours later by a warm, wet feeling in my groin. I opened my eyes to see that Chuck was down at the bottom of the bed and he was giving me a slow blowjob, my body started to tense-up.

Just as Chuck realized that I was awake he deep throated my stiff cock, clear down to my hair and slowly sucked his way back up, until he slowly licking the head of my cock. The sensation felt soon good that I let out a load moan and my body started to shake. I was getting close to cumming again. Suddenly, Chuck stopped sucking my cock and he grabbed the head of my cock and squeezed it hard.

"Hold on sweet cheeks, no fair cumming. You will need your load for the video interview."

I just looked at Chuck as he kneeled over me firmly holding the tip of my cock and I said, "Video interview, what's that?"

"It's a chance for you to show your stuff on film and to see how you will look."

I smiled, and just said, "O.K."

With that Chuck took me by the hands and pulled me off the bed. He put his arms around me with his hands firmly grabbing my bare ass.

"Well Jimmy, don't bother getting dressed, while I set up the video equipment go into the kitchen and fix us some soup and toast. I kissed him and smiled.

"Yes Sir, I'll have it ready in no time.

It became apparent rather fast that Chuck enjoyed seeing me walk around his house in the nude. Several times while I was fixing something to eat he would walk into the kitchen and give me a deep kiss as he either played with my ass or fondled me. Both of which I enjoyed as much as he did.

It took us about a half hour to eat our meal. After our little meal Chuck gave me a pair of walking shorts, a football jersey, some tennis shoes and gym socks to wear for the video interview. During the shoot, as Chuck called it, I would just sit in a high back chair in the bedroom, talk to Chuck about myself and then strip down and slowly beat off. When it came to exactly what I was to say I was a little confused, but Chuck said, "Don't worry, you can just wing it. You will do all right. I will guide you through it."

I was already learning to trust Chuck's judgment, after all he was the expert and I was eager to get started.

When Chuck had the set ready he called me into the bedroom. "Jimmy did you review the questions, as I told you too?"

"Yes Sir, I know what to say."

Chuck looked pleased. I was told to sit in the high back chair and look directly at the camera. Chuck than adjusted the lighting and tested some equipment. We were ready to go and best of all I was not nervous.

Chuck sat in a small chair next to the camera and looked at me and smiled, "Well Jimmy, are you ready to begin?"

"Yes Sir, I'm ready."

Chuck turned on the camera and he started to ask me some basic questions. "What is your name and where are you from?"

"My name is James, but people call me Jimmy and I grew up in a small town in Ohio."

"How old are you Jimmy?"

"I am 19 years old."

"Wow, you are just barely legal."

What followed were questions about my boyhood and what I liked about it and what I hated. I don't know why but the idea of being in front of a camera was starting to turn me on, my cock was already half hard and I could feel a surge of sexual energy flowing though my body.

"Well Jimmy, you have had an interesting boyhood. Now let's see what you look like naked."

"O.K. so you want me to strip."

"Yes, that's the general idea."

I took off my tennis shoes and socks first and then my shirt and shorts. When I sat down in again in the chair my cock was already hard and throbbing up and down.

"Well Jimmy, I see that you are eager to show off your big piece of meat. How big is your cock?"

"It's 9 and one half inches, by 7 inches."

"Would you consider your big cock to be your best point?"

"No, I have been told that I have a good body and a cute ass."

"Can you show us that cute ass of yours?"

I did not say a word I just smiled and got up from the chair and turned around exposing my ass to the camera.

"Wow, you do have a cute ass. Could you bend over and give us a better view?"

I just followed Chuck's instructions and then sat down again. My cock was now throbbing wildly up and down. I was starting to really get into the whole scene.

"Well Jimmy, let's see you stroke your big cock for us."

"O.K."

I grabbed a tube of Lube and put a liberal amount on my now rock hard cock and I started to slowly beat my meat.

"How does that feel Jimmy?"

"Wild, it is really starting to turn me on."

After I had stroked my cock for several minutes I had to stop and squeeze the head of my dick really hard.

"Well Jimmy you nearly lose your load, didn't you?"

I laughed a little and half smiled. "Yes, I'm very horny today."

"I noticed that you had to squeeze the head of your dick to stop from cumming, is that the only way you can do it?"

"Yes, once my cock starts to build up to cumming I can't stop it any other way."

"You mean that if you stopped beating your meat and didn't touch yourself at all that you would still shoot a big load?"

"Yes, that is true. I can't stop from cumming any other way."

"How about showing us what would happen if you didn't squeeze the head of your cock when you are close to cumming. Let's see you cum without touching yourself."

I just smiled at the camera. This was going to be wild. I started to slowly stroke my cock and in only about a minute I was past the point of no return. I let go of my cock and it throbbed up and down for almost another minute, as my face tensed-up, my body started to shake and finally my eyes started to roll back until I was looking at the ceiling. My cock just erupted and shot stream after stream of warm, sticky cum several feet into the air. As my body violently shook, globs of cum spattered down on my squirming, naked body. When my cock was spent I looked at the camera and smiled.

With cum dripping off my face and body my cock stayed hard and throbbing, with streams of cum slowing dripping down its sides. Chuck's camera got a close up shot of all of it, included my throbbing cum covered cock.

After Chuck filmed his close up shots I ran my fingers over my face and body scooping up my cum before I started to slowly lick it off my fingers, like it was a great tasting dessert, as I smiled at the camera. Chuck did not say a word he just kept filming until I had licked up every drop. Chuck than gave me a towel to clean off my body and fingers.

"Wow that was some show I have never seen anyone cum like that before and then lick themselves clean."

Chuck had a short-term loss of words at this point. He eyes were fixed on me. Then he suddenly got back his composure.

"How many times can you cum in one day?"

"If I wanted to I could get off 10 or more in a day."

"How many times do you cum per day on average?"

"While I can cum again and again, every day, I don't need to. I can get by with just once a month if I have too."

"Unlike most young men you seem to be able to control your cock, rather than the other way around. What is your biggest sexual fantasy?"

"I would have to say that my biggest fantasy is to be the top gay porn star in the business, so that I can get fucked by porn studs for a living."

Chuck just smiled, ear to ear. He didn't have to say it' I had the job.

CHAPTER NINE

GARY

Departing from O'Hara Air Bus Terminal, in Chicago, was easier and faster than our arrival. From taxi to Air Bus only took us about an hour. I was looking forward to this flight. This would be my first time on the new anti-gravity Air Bus. The flight to New York City was comfortable and fast.

On our arrival in New York City air space the Air Bus circled the city once to give the passengers a great view of the city skyline. The Air Bus than set down vertically, at a new air terminal, only a few miles from the city.

The trip by taxi into New York City did not go as well as our trip. The trip was a mass of delays, from trying to talk to the driver, who did not speak much English, to getting stuck in rush hour traffic. It took our taxi driver three hours to drop us off at our hotel in downtown New York. When we got to our room we both undressed and slept for a few hours. This was the best period of a taxing day for me. I love to cuddle up naked with my master and sleep next to him, with my head on his chest and his arm across my back.

After a few hours of sleep my master kicked the covers off the bed and slapped me on my bare ass. It was time for us to get up. We took a quick shower and got dressed to go out to dinner. My master told me to put on some old jeans, a pair of tennis shoes and a t-shirt, while he wore old jeans, boots and an old work shirt.

My master had not told me much about the prospect that he was to interview and possibly sign, except that he was 20 years old and his name was Gary. All other facts about Gary and what we were to do in New York, my master chose to keep to himself.

All I knew about the next few hours was that my master was hungry and we were going to dinner. After only walking a few blocks my master chose to eat at a Chinese restaurant. Since it was only 6:00 P.M., my master and I killed the next two hours having a good meal and watching the foot traffic outside the restaurant. At 8:00 P.M. my master paid the bill and I followed him out the door. Where we were going was known only to my master and it was not my place to ask questions about such things.

After walking about ten blocks my master stopped. He looked across the street at a theater and turned to me and said, "Well Boy let's try out a strip joint."

"Yes Sir!" The theater was a gay strip club named, The All Male Review. As my master bought the tickets I wondered what it was like in one of these places. I had never been to any type of strip club before.

The 9:00 P.M. show had not started yet and the theater was just starting to fill up. My master picked out two seats near the end of the performance runway that had no seats in front of them. We sat down and waited about 15 minutes for the show to start.

At 9:15 P.M. the lights in the theater slowly went out only to be replaced by stage and runway lighting. With background music playing an announcer opened the show by welcoming everybody to the show and then proceeded to describe the four young men who would be performing that night.

The first stripper was a young Asian man named Kevin. He did a slow strip tease number to an old fashion Rap Music background. His body was a basic smooth skinned, swimmers build, a boyish face and about an 8 inch cock. The audience seemed to like this stripper, especially when he worked his way through the audience, wearing only his socks. People would put money into his socks as he did a little more private entertaining in front of their seats. The announcer at the start of the show told the audience that people could not fondle or have sex with the performers, but you could play with their asses, caress their bodies and they could kiss you if they wanted. This stripper never came close to either my master or me, he targeted old men and they filled his socks full of bills. My master said that the old men are the best tippers and young men tend to be cheap, so some strippers just go after the older men in the audience, this way of performing wasn't as much fun for a stripper, but it was far more profitable.

The second stripper was a young Hispanic man of about 25 years of age. He was more muscular and better defined than the first stripper. Unlike the first stripper, this young man paid a lot of attention to my master and me. He did a private show in front of our seats that had people in the audience walking over to stand closer to our seats, in order to get a better look. It was a strange feeling for me to have a naked stripper sit on my lap and kiss me on the cheek, while his hard, throbbing cock bounced against my stomach. My master just looked at us and smiled. My jeans had started to develop a serious bulge problem. My master thought that the whole thing was rather funny. After this stripper did the same act on my master's lap he put several bills into his socks and the stripper kissed him on the lips and said. "Thank you Sir!"

The third stripper was the headliner of the show. He was young white boy, with short blond hair, smooth skin and an extremely muscular and well-defined body. This stripper had a teenager's face and a man's body. Half way through his act he played a tensing game with his shorts, slowly exposing his ass. When he finally dropped his shorts, the audience gasped. The boy had an incredible looking ass. For the next few minutes he danced with only his socks on and a towel in front of his cock.

Finally, he dropped the towel and you could hear moans and sounds of clapping from the audience. He must have had at least 9 inches of man meat between his legs. Looking at his cute face, muscular body and huge cock, it was easy to see why this stripper was the show's headliner. This stripper not only was the favorite of the audience, he seemed to attract the attention of my master too. I smiled as I watched my master's eyes follow the stripper. It pleased me to know that my master was fascinated by this performer, since he was physically a lot like me.

After the headliner had finished his show on the stage he came down into the audience to do more personal shows for individuals in the audience and of course rack up some tips. The young man made the rounds and collected a lot of bills in his socks before he walked over to start to perform in front of my master and me. My master visually inspected the boy's naked body and very hard cock. He smiled, he seemed to be pleased.

The boy didn't pay much attention to me, I guess likes don't attract likes, but he did pay attention to my master. This dancer made quite a fuss over him. The audience sensed that something special was happening and they started to get out of their chairs and walk over to stand near us, in order to get a better look at the action.

The young stripper did his individual show in front of my master's chair and then he started to get more personal. While dancing he would stop at times to start to unbutton my master's shirt. When he had my master's muscular chest exposed the stripper sat on his lap, facing him and let his big throbbing cock, bounce up and down on his chest, while he gave my master a deep and long kiss that had the audience clapping and moaning. The boy than got up and started to dance and play with my master's face as he threw kisses at him. The audience laughed and clapped and my master put some bills in the stripper's socks. The stripper bent down and kissed my master one more time and then he left, his part of the show was over.

The next stripper was a good-looking young white boy of about 25 years of age. He had a semi-hairy, muscular body and a definite flair for dancing. His act was the best-staged act of the show. Half way through the act my master looked at his watch and motioned for me to follow him outside. The show was over for us, my master wanted to leave.

As we left the theater I looked over to the left of us and saw the blond stripper, who had headlined the show leaning against the front of the theater. As my master and I passed him my master raised his right hand and snapped his fingers. The young man just fell in line behind my master and did not say a work. He just devotedly looked at my master and smiled. So, this was Gary.

My master led us both down the street for several blocks, before he turned into an alley. He seemed to know exactly where he was going. The alley dead-ended at what looked like a warehouse. My master snapped his fingers again and the new boy came forward and used his key to open the door to the warehouse.

The interior of this part of the warehouse had been converted into an apartment. The walls were old brick, the floor and ceiling was wood, and a staircase that led upstairs was metal. On one of the exposed brick walls was a huge 12 foot by 8 foot, wall T.V. unit. The apartment was finished in a confused mix of modern and old style furniture. The place was designed for comfort not show. My master showed no interest in the apartment. He acted like he had been here before.

My master was in a business mood and he ordered both of us to strip. We quickly followed his orders and we were soon standing naked, with a submissive posture, in the middle of the apartment living room. My master than ordered me to sit down in front of one of the nearby chairs and just watch and listen, he then started to inspect the new boy's naked body. The inspection proceeded without any problems, the new boy seemed to check out and my master was pleased with him. The new boy seemed to like being man-handled by my master's strong hands, his huge cock was now throbbing hard.

My master was though with his inspection of the new boy's body and he walked over by one of the living room chairs and started to take off his clothes. I sat on the floor eagerly watching my master slowly take off his clothes and put them on the chair. My cock was getting rock hard. I know that my master was getting really for some action and I was silently praying that he would include me in his plans.

After my master took off his last item of clothes he started to walk around the new boy who was standing naked and silent, with his head bowed and his hands behind his back, in the middle of the living room. The new boy could see that my master was naked and his half-hard cock rose to a full and throbbing erection. The boy was hoping for some action and so was I.

After walking several laps around the new boy, my master stopped behind him and ordered the boy to turn around and face him. I was now ordered to join the new boy. As we both stood in front of my master, with roaring hard-ons, a fact that seems to interest my master, my master silently stared at us for several minutes. Finally, he told both of us what he wanted us to do. "Listen up Boys; you are now going to sexually please your master. I want you to work together and work your way down my body, as I direct you. Do you understand what you are to do?"

"Yes Sir!"

"Now come forward and make out with your master."

"Yes Sir!"

We both stepped forward, one on each side and we started to kiss our master on his face. After only a few minutes he grabbed us both by the hair on the back of our heads and directed our efforts down to his neck and then up to his ear lobes. While we both licked and softly bit his ear lobes, our master grabbed us again by the hair and forced the new boy's head down to work on one of his nipples, while my master pulled my head back and started to make out with me. While my master and I made out he played with my bare ass, while he stroked the new boy's cock, causing us both to softly moan and squirm.

Just as I was getting so turned-on that I was getting close to cumming my master pulled my head back and squeezed the head of my cock, until I my cock relaxed. He then switched our positions. I started to work on one of his nipples as my master make out with the new boy.

In few minutes my master had us both working on his nipples and licking our way up and around his armpits. He started to moan and squirm a little and his cock got hard and started to throb up and down. My master was enjoying his little show.

As our little performance continued we both were directed down my master's body to lick and kiss his balls and to take turns at sucking his beautiful cock. The longer we both worked on my master's cock the more turned-on his got, but we were not allowed to get him off, he had other plans for his cock.

Suddenly, my master yanked us both off of his cock and pulled us onto our feet. He held us by the hair on the back of our heads as he took turns giving us each a long and deep kiss before he released us. As my master backed away from us we assumed a submissive stance and we waited for my master to have further use for us.

My master stood silently for a moment, looking at the both of us, as if he were thinking, before he ordered me to go sit on the floor next to the wall and just watch. I softly moaned, thinking that my master had no further use for me.

As I sat down next to the wall my master told the new boy to turn around. He quickly obeyed. My master now picked up a large couch pillow and threw it on the floor, opened a door on the coffee table, and took out a jar of Lube and a towel. He put the jar and towel on the floor and then walked over to the new boy and started to run his hands over his naked backside. As my master played with the boy's ass he started to smile, he knew that he was going to get fucked.

My master now ordered the boy to bend over and spread his legs. The boy moaned and his legs shook as my master shoved several greased fingers up his ass. After the boy had settled down he was ordered to lie on the floor, with the couch pillow under his hips and his ass in the air. Before his body had time to settle on the floor my master slid his cock deep into the boy's ass. The boy's upper body lifted off the floor and his let out a loud moan, as his whole body shook.

In just a few minutes the boy had adjusted to the thrust of my master's cock and he started to smile and softly moan. He was really enjoying this fucking. This boy was a natural bottom.

As my master gently and violently fucked the new boy, I closed my eyes and tried to imagine that I was the new boy. After a while I could just about feel my master's cock thrusting in and out of my ass. It felt so good I almost started to cum.

My master fucked the new boy for about a good half hour, before his body started to tense up and he grit his teeth and shot a big load up the boy's ass. The boy moaned as my master withdrew his cock and slapped the boy's bare ass several times. This is the way my master has of saying that you were a good fuck.

As my master got to his feet sweat was running down his body. He looked at me and then pointed at the towel. I quickly got up and grabbed the towel and I started to rub down my master's naked body. When I was done my master smiled at me and said, "O.K. Boy, it's your turn to fuck the new boy."

"Yes Sir!"

I walked over to the coffee table, grabbed the jar of Lube, and started to grease up my now throbbing hard man cock. I looked down at the new boy he was looking at my big cock and smiling, ear to ear. I know this look. It is the look that you see on a hung bottom's face, when they know that they are going to find out what it's like to get fucked by a cock as big as theirs. The new boy was finally going to do what super hung bottoms only dream about, he was going to fuck himself.

My master had just given me the new boy's ass and I was determined to give my master a good show. After greasing up my cock I put the jar of Lube down on the coffee table and walked over to stand between the legs of the new boy, who looked up at my throbbing, greased cock and smiled. I bend down, slapped his ass really hard, and said, "Boy, get on your knees and hands, doggy style."

"Yes Sir!"

The boy quickly obeyed and I parted his ass cheeks and positioned the head of my big cock against his asshole. I leaned forward, the boy let out a loud moan and his body shook, as my big cock slid deep into his ass.

After giving the boy's ass a few minutes to adjust to the probing thrusts of my cock, I put my hands on his shoulders and started to really shove it to him. The first really deep thrust of my cock caused the boy's upper body to lift off the ground and he moaned so loud that he almost screamed. He soon adjusted to the full-length thrusts of my big cock and he started to encourage me. "Yes, yes, fuck me Sir, Fuck me really hard." As I picked up speed the boy moaned and his upper body would buck off the ground with each deep thrust. I was starting to fuck the new boy the same way may master fucks me, and both of us were really getting into it.

I fucked the boy hard and deep on his knees for about 10 minutes when my master ordered me to put the boy on his back. I turned the boy over on his back, put his legs on my shoulders and raised his ass off the floor. The first full thrust of my big cock at this new angle sent the boy into a moaning fit. The boy spread his arms out to his sides and he started to violently shake and moan louder and louder. The boy's huge cock was rapidly moving up and down and the boy started to grit his teeth, he was getting close to cumming.

My master now leaned forward in his chair and said, "O.K. Boys let's see both of you cum." Both the boy and I didn't need any more encouragement. As my body was starting to tense up

I felt the boy's ass tighten up, as he let out a loud scream, just as his huge cock started to shoot a big load of cum all over his face and upper body. As the boy's cock started to relax my body tensed up and I withdrew my throbbing cock from the boy's ass and let it freely unload stream after stream of warm, sticky cum on the boy's already cum covered upper body.

After my cock was spent, I looked at the new boy, he was smiling. The boy had enjoyed my little show. I leaned forward, grabbed both of his nipples, and twisted them really hard. The boy boy's eyes got really big and he screamed. I let go of the boy's nipples and smiled at him. This boy was not only a good fuck he is also fun to play with. My master will be proud to own a property like him.

After we cleaned up, the new boy and I spent the rest of the evening sitting naked at the feet of my master, watching a movie on the big wall T.V. During intermissions my master would play with his two boys, which kept our cocks hard, though out the whole movie.

The new boy and I spent that night sleeping naked next to my master, one of us on each side of him. The next morning the new boy signed papers and became the latest property of my master. I felt a sense of relief, my master's trip to inspect and sign a second house slave was about over, we were now going home.

CHAPTER TEN

MY DARK SIDE

Everyone has a dark side that will come to the surface at different times in their lives, like a wild beast that needs some sort of attention, or to just be fed some form of nourishment. Most people learn to deal with these hidden desires, mainly because they are usually considered anti-social in nature, or just plain illegal. I am no different, my dark side has always has been concerned with being nude and maybe even shocking in public, my dick gets hard just thinking about it.

Most young, gay males, with chronic exhibitionist tendencies like me, and a drop dead gorgeous body would satisfy their cravings by doing something like working as a male stripper, posing for a centerfold, or becoming a gay porn star. But, due to the fact that I am from a prominent, wealthy and very conservative family, I have had to find other ways to deal with my kinky nature.

One such way keeps me content on a weekly basis. I work out intensely three times a week.

But, what makes it a real turn on is the location and way that I exercise.

I have my own exercise room in a very upper class, modern apartment. Thank god for all that family money. The room is well equipped and has a big floor to ceiling window that has a view of the apartment building across the street. My neighbors are mostly gay males and I know many of them have a set of binoculars and at least one has a star gazing telescope.

I can usually tell when I am being watched. When people are playing peeping tom games they don't want to be seen, so they will turn off the light in the room that they are using and sit in the dark while they watch me exercise and strip. It is almost like taking a viewer poll, the more lights that click off the larger my audience.

I make my exercise nights and time predictable, but what I will do is not. My regular routine nights start at 8:00 P.M. Before I start my routine I turn the temperature in my exercise room up to 90 degrees. I exercise hard until my sweat clothes are all wet and then I strip off my sweatshirt and slowly do pull ups, flexing every muscle. I have a very muscular, extremely defined upper body and I can just feel the eyes inspecting every small section of my torso. The sensation of knowing that I am being watched can cause me to get an erection.

But, one or two nights a month it can get much more interesting. When I'm in one of my strange, kinky moods, I will exercise while I slowly do a strip act. At this point the prick tease part of my dark side takes over. My sweatshirt will come off after the first set is complete. By the time I get to the end of my exercise routine I am covered in sweat and my big cock is arching to be released from the only clothes that I still have on, my jock strap. Now I will get ready to do my pull-ups by turning my back to the window and striping off my jock strap, while bending over to show off my asshole in the process. Then I reached up, grab the overhead bar, and start to do behind the neck pull-ups. My audience gets a great view of my beautiful, rounded, firm ass and my extremely muscular back, as I repeatedly pull my shoulders up to touch the bar. Next, I let go of the bar and drop to my feet and turned around, exposing my throbbing hard cock, just before I started to do frontal pull-ups, slowly pulling my naked body up until my upper chest touches the bar. With each pull-up my big, stiff cock will throb wildly up and down as if it is doing its own set of exercises. I can just feel my sex hunger neighbors licking beads of sweat off my naked body.

But, naked pull-ups are not the end of my act, for a hot finish I sit in an exercise chair facing the window, lean back and slowly stroke my throbbing cock until my body tenses up and starts to tremble. Than when I am ready, all I have to do is to fantasize that one of my horny young neighbors is kneeling naked between my legs and licking the sweat off my balls. That is all it takes before I let out a loud moan and shoot a big load all over my sweat covered chest and stomach. Then I just sit still for a moment as my body relaxes before I get up and walk over to the bathroom door and turn off the lights in the exercise room.

My little public show is now over, but I am not always through with my own performance. As I take a badly needed shower I will sometimes continue to fantasize about all those horny guys with binoculars that have just beaten off watching my little show. That thought is enough to get my cock hard again and I finish my shower by shooting one more load against the tile walls of my shower.

But, once a year I just have to really cut loose and do something bold and possibly shocking. The last time I had such an overwhelming urge to show off I flew to my old college town and checked into the baths. I did the needed research on how to act out my little fantasy and I had prepared my body for the task.

I choose to rent a large room, with a double bed, several hours before the main crowd usually arrives. This was the first Saturday night after college mid-terms and it was gym night. A lot of gym toned, very horny college studs and their friends were sure to show up.

After sleeping for about 3 hours I awoke to the sounds of voices and heavy foot traffic in the hallway outside my room. Show time had arrived. I got up, turned on the light and then started to do a few simple stretching exercises in the nude to wake up my body.

After my muscles were warmed up and flexible I reach into my overnight bag and pulled out my collar. After fastening the one-inch, silver, choke chain around my neck I stopped to look at myself in the full-length mirror on the back of the room's door.

The transformation was striking. I had cut my blond hair short, in a more military style. My almost smooth naked body had been completely shaved of body hair from the neck down and a two-inch silver cock ring dangled from the end of my thick 8-inch cock. The silver chain slave collar really looked good on my pale, tan less, 5 foot, 10 inch, muscular, well-defined body. I finished my self-inspection by turning around and running my hands over the firm mounds of my hairless ass and said, "Man, it has been too long. I just have to get my pretty ass plowed by a hung stud tonight."

I had the look that would attract a lot of attention, even up against all the hot young studs that were should to show up at the baths tonight. Hell, I doubt even experienced leather masters had ever seem a sight like me.

Tonight, I am my master's, well-trained slave and he has just dropped me off at the baths to play as I pleased, as a reward for past service. All that is left for me to do is act out the part.

I took a deep breath, opened the door, and started to walk naked down the hallway. The reaction of the bathhouse crowd was encouraging. People stared at me, some in disbelief and others with approving smiles. I walked past them, my eyes fixed forward and with no expression on my face. I could feel their eyes inspecting every inch of my naked slave body. No one said a word to me. The reaction of the crowd started to turn me on and my big cock began to get hard.

By the time I reached the stairs my cock was throbbing hard and it started bouncing up and down as I walked down the stairs to the first floor. I walked the halls of both floors of the bathhouse twice, not stopping, or really looking at any of the people. I wasn't there to be social or polite. I was my master's slave and I was available to please as many young studs as possible.

It did not take me long to find out where the really studs were hanging out and I decided to check out the place. I walked into large, semi-dark orgy room. A very muscular, light skinned, young black man was fucking a red haired young stud, on a round bed, in the middle of the room. When he spotted me he stopped fucking his partner for a brief moment as he looked over my naked body from my head to my toes. He then gave me a long hunger stare, as if he would rather be fucking me.

As the crowd of mostly young men started to notice me standing near the entrance to the room, I quickly picked out three good-looking, nicely hung men in the back of the room. They were naked and leaning against the back wall, stroking their stiff cocks, as they watched the two men fucking on the round bed. The man in the middle was a dark haired, rugged looking stud, of about his early 30's. To his right was a red-haired, semi-butch, very defined, man of about the same age and the third man was much younger than his two friends. He was a pretty, young, blond stud of about 19 or 20 years of age. They all sported cocks that were around 8 inches.

I stood still and stared at them until they noticed me. Just after their eyes met mine and they gave me a very startled, but approving look, I walked over, knelt down in front of their throbbing cocks, and said, "Please Sirs, may I suck your cocks?"

None of them said a word to me, as the three of them took a step forward to stand within inches of my face. I leaned forward and quickly swallowed the middle studs cock almost down to his pubes. As I repeatedly deep throated his cock I started to fondle the other two men and after only a minute or so I started to switch from one cock to another. The way their bodies reacted to my performance told me that they were very pleased with me. A crowd started to form around us as I got the three young men closer and closer to shooting their loads.

The young, blond stud was the first to act like he was getting close and I stopped sucking his cock for a brief moment and looked up and said, "Please Sir, will you shoot your load on my body?"

He nodded and I swallowed his cock almost down to his hair several times before he moaned, withdrew his cock from my mouth, stroked it a few times and then shot a big load of thick, warm cum on my chest. The other two studs soon followed suit, one shooting off on my face and neck and the other dropped his load on my back. I smiled, stroked each of their spent cocks and thanked them.

As the three studs left the room, I looked around to see that I was the center of attraction. About 20 men were staring at me and stroking their hard cocks. I just smiled and said, "Sirs, do any of you want to shoot your loads on me?"

With that announcement, several naked men quickly surrounded me. As I knelt submissively on the floor I slowly stroked my cock, stopping each time I got close to cumming. Each time that I felt warm, sticky cum spatter on some part of my body I would say, "Thank you, Sir!"

This sign of submission seemed to give other men in the room the encouragement they needed to step forward and release their loads all over my naked body.

This whole wild scene had really turned me on both mentally and sexually. My big cock was standing almost straight up and felt hard as a brick. Part of my plan for this night was that I would not allow myself to cum. I wanted to stay sexually on edge all the night in order, to conserve energy and to get as much of a mental rush as possible. Well, at least that was my plan.

The cum of over 10 men was dripping down almost all parts of my naked body, as I walked slowly out of the orgy room and down the hall. This time the motion of simply walking down the stairs had unplanned consequences.

With each downward step my throbbing cock started to bounce up and down, causing an erotic chain reaction that quickly had me getting closer and closer to cumming. By the time I had reached the ground floor my body was beginning to tense up and I knew it was too late to stop the process. I just stopped walking and closed my eyes. The erotic tension in my groin rose so rapidly that my big cock throbbed upward one more time and then stream after stream of thick cum shoot several feet into the air. I let out a soft moan and my body jerked each time my cock erupted.

After my cock was spent my body started to relax and I opened my eyes to see that about a dozen men were staring at me with a very startled look on their faces. I had planned this evening in great detail and I tried to predict all possibilities, this event was unplanned and it really startled me. I just stood there frozen in time. Suddenly, someone in the crowd started to clap his hands and say, "Great show, man."

Soon almost all of the men in the hallway were clapping and smiling. A little embarrassed, I just smiled and started to walk down the hall.

I took a nice warm shower and quickly toweled off, before I headed for my room. After I had gotten about an hour or so of sleep I heard a knock on the door and I got up. When I opened the door I saw a very attractive man leaning against the opposite wall. He just stared at me. I looked him over and smiled.

The man was about 30 years old. He had a handsome face and a very muscular, well-defined upper body. Suddenly, the man pulled on his towel and let it drop to the floor. My jaw just dropped. Wooooo, is that real. I was staring at over 10 inches of prime stud meat.

The man now walked over to my room and put his hands on the top of the doorframe. With his face only inches from mine he smiled and said, "Well Slave, how would you like to be royally fucked by a super hung top?"

I just nodded my head and motioned for him to enter the room. My strange and wild night was about to take another unplanned, but this time, a very welcomed turn.

CHAPTER ELEVEN

THE SHOT

It was about 7 A.M. in the morning when I awoke to the feel of my new lover's hand caressing my back. As I lifted my head off of the pillow and turned to face my lover he smiled and said, "Well sweet cheeks, this is your big day. How do you feel?"

I rubbed my eyes and smiled, "I'm a little nervous, but eager to get started."

"I know how to handle first day nervous problems." He then kicked the covers off the bed and took away my pillow.

"Now just put your head down on the bed and your hands at your sides. I am going to give you a relaxing massage and get some of that tension out of your body."

I did just as I was told. Chuck quickly sat down on my ass with his big cock touching the lower part of my back. A spark of sexual tension flashed threw my body and my now hard cock throbbed a little.

Chuck now proceeded to firmly massage my body, starting with my neck and working his way down my back and back up again. After about 15 minutes of expertly massaging my neck, shoulders and back. Chuck lifted off of my body and stood on the side of the bed as he started to work on my right leg, as his now rock hard cock repeatedly throbbed up and down. When he got to my foot he started to work on pressure points. Each time that he really dug into a pressure point my body would tense up and I started to moan.

"Oh gooood, ahhh!"

After about a half hour of the most relaxing massage that I have ever had, Chuck was done. He then slapped my bare ass.

"O.K. sweet cheeks get up we have to get ready for the shoot."

When I was up and standing next to the bed, Chuck noticed that I had a big, throbbing hard-on.

"Well, sweet cheeks you are eager to get started." He then grabbed me by my hard dick and led me into the bathroom.

After I had finished shaving off the few whiskers that I have on my boyish face I turned around to look at myself in the mirror on the back of the bathroom door. As Chuck continued to brush his teeth I looked over my naked body in the mirror. Jesus, my friend Hank is right I am a chicken hawk's wet dream. The reflection in the mirror was of a smooth bodied, hung, blond, pretty boy, with a muscular swimmer's build. As I started to play with my own balls I realized that today I was going to sell this pretty, naked body of mine to thousands of strangers. The whole idea startled me a little, but strangely, it really started to turn me on. It seems my lover Chuck is right, I am porn star material.

While Chuck finished up in the bathroom I walked into the bedroom and started to down some exercises to limber up a little more. When Chuck walked into the bedroom I was doing pushups with my nearly soft cock rubbing the carpet each time that I lowered my body almost to the floor.

"Well Babe, I'm in the mood to show you a more interesting way to do pushups."

Without waiting for a reply Chuck got under my hips and he started to lick my balls each time I lowered my body towards the floor. The feel of his warm tough on my firm balls caused my cock to firm up and throb like I was an animal in heat.

As I reached the count of seventeen pushups Chuck slid my cock into his mouth and starting to suck my throbbing cock. The duel sensation of the pleasure of my cock being sucked by an expert and the intense pain in my arms, I almost lost my load.

Before I reached the no return point Chuck pulled my cock out of his mouth and gripping both sides of my hips he rolled me over on my back. As my body relaxed Chuck sat on my hips and leaned down, to a point in which his face was nearly touching mine. I got something for you babe. My lover now stood up on his knees and he leaned forward. I was face to face with a throbbing hard cock. I looked up at my lover's smiling face the game was not over yet. I knew an invitation when I see one staring in the face. I buried my face in my lover's crotch and started to eagerly lick his big, firm, hairless balls. The scent and taste of his crotch started to drive my already hard cock wild.

After not being allowed to cum in over a week I was super horny and my hungry tongue and mouth just bathed my lover's balls in warm saliva. My lover's body squirmed and he moaned.

"Damn you're good at that."

As I proceeded to tongue his big cock, from its hairy base to its plump head, his cock started to pulsate up and down, as if it was playing a game with my tongue. When I swallowed his cock almost down to its base my lover started to rapidly moan and his body tensed up. His moaning grew louder as I continued to deep throat his rock hard cock. Just as I moved my hands down to massage the sides of his feet my lover pulled his cock out of my mouth and squeezed its head hard.

"Damn it, you know that tickling the sides of my feet will send me over the edge. I have to save this load for the shoot today."

He smiled and patted me on the head. "Sorry Babe, I can't let you have it right now."

My lover than reached down and slapped my bare ass.

"Well, sweet cheeks time to shower. We have to get ready for the shoot."

It had only been two months since I followed the advice of my friend Hank to do an interview to be a porn star, so that I could get some extra income to pay off my debts. Hank arranged the interview and it seems I really impressed the owner of the firm company, porn star Chuck Wade. He not only gave me the job he became my lover. He also signed me to a three-picture deal. Today, we are going to shoot the first scene of the new flick.

The location of the shoot was at a private home in the Hollywood Hills. When we got to the address Chuck pulled off the road into a tree-lined driveway that led to an iron gate. Chuck honked the car horn twice and the gate started to open. Inside the gate was a small parking lot that was big enough for only four cars.

As the car came to a halt, Chuck turned to me and smiled, "OK. Babe lets go." He had that gleam in his eyes that I was starting to believe meant that he was proud of me.

As we approached the house I could see that it was a simple one-story building with a pool in the backyard. The owner of the house came out to greet us. Chuck introduced us, "Jimmy I would like you to meet Mr. Johnson."

Mr. Johnson was a stocky man with a short, well-trimmed beard. I figured him to be about in his 60's. I stepped forward and shook his hand.

"It's nice to meet you Mr. Johnson."

The man smiled, "It's good to meet you too. You can just call me Jesse, everyone else does."

Mr. Johnson than turned to look at Chuck, "Well Chuck, so is this sexy young man is your new porn star?"

Chuck managed a slight smile. "If you think he is sexy now Jesse just wait until you see him buck naked. He will really blow your socks off."

Mr. Johnson started to smile a little. "Hell, at my age such a welcomed sight could be more of a health risk than a turn-on. But I'm more than willing to take the risk."

We both followed Mr. Johnson into his house and he told us to make ourselves comfortable in the living room. As we sat down on a large leather sofa two more men entered the room.

"Hi Chuck."

"Well, it is good to see that you two found the house without any trouble."

"Hey, have faith man."

The second man than cut in, "It was easy finding Jesse's place, we have both been here many times for some Jesse's famous dinner parties and we have helped film many porn flicks here too."

Chuck now introduced me. "Jimmy I would like you to meet Noll and Rick, two of the best camera men in the porn business."

As I shook hands with both of the men they looked me over as if they were undressing me. I blushed a little. Back home in Ohio I seldom got such attention, except in the school shower room and never when I was looking directly at the person. Being some sort of sex object was a new feeling to me. The whole scene made me a little nervous.

After filming the introduction scenes, the ones where we have are clothes on, we were ready for the first sex scene. The scene was set in the living room. The cameramen set up their equipment and quickly shot a scene of both me and Chuck coming into the house. When we got to the living room the action stopped while the crew rearranged the cameras and lights.

After the crew was ready the cameras started to roll again. As we both stood in the living room Chuck looked into my eyes, grabbed me by my collar, pulled my head forward, and gave me a long deep kiss. My cock quickly got rock hard. Chuck and I than started to get undressed in stages, as we kissed and played with our bodies, until we were both standing naked, cock to cock, in the middle of the room.

After several minutes of making out with me as our cocks throbbed against each other Chuck started to kiss and lick his way down my naked body. He started with my neck and ear lobes and he proceeded down until he was licking and lightly biting my nipples.

"Ahh… God that feels good."

He then lifted up my left arm and started to lick the sides of my arm pit just before he ran his tongue through my arm pit several times. My body tensed up and I moaned. The cameramen got not only shots of Chuck and his great tongue action, but also shots of my facial expressions.

At this point the cameramen yelled cut and the action stopped. Chuck gave me a light kiss, "Good work so far Babe."

My lover then walked over to his backpack and put on a pair of gym shorts, before he disappeared into a back room with one of the cameramen.

I was left standing naked, with a throbbing hard-on, in the middle of the living room. The other cameraman just stared at me, looking over my naked body, like I was a piece of raw meat and he was a hungry animal. It all made me very nervous. I quickly got a pair of shorts from my lover's backpack to put on.

The cameraman than said, "We will be filming again in about 15 minutes. Chuck and Noll are looking over the scene."

He then added, "You know you do have a great body and if you are interested, after the shoot is over, both Noll and I will give you $300 bucks if we can both fuck your pretty ass."

I don't know how, maybe it was the sexual tension in the air, but when Chuck came back for the next scene I still had a throbbing hard-on. Maybe, it was because Chuck had not let me cum in over a week.

In the next scene Chuck licked his way down to my cock and he started to lick my balls as he slowly stroked my throbbing hard cock. As started to moan louder and louder I pulled on Chuck's ear, which was a sign that I was close to cumming. Chuck stopped licking my balls and yelled cut.

As he squeezed the head of my cock really tight, he looked up at me.

"Babe, you nearly lost it, didn't you."

He just smiled. "It's all par for the course. You are really horny, just the way I want you to be."

He seemed pleased with me and that helped a lot.

We finished that part of the scene with Chuck sucking my Cock, which had me so turned on that I had to stop the scene twice, in order to keep from shooting my load. We than had an hour-long break, while Chuck looked over the film and Mr. Johnson was nice enough to fix something for me to eat.

The final part of the scene had me draped over an ottoman, with my knees on the floor and Chuck eating my ass. Chuck's talented tongue had me moaning and squirming so violently that he had some trouble keeping his tongue up my ass. In this scene one cameraman was in front of me filming my facial and body reactions and the other cameraman was filming Chuck and my big throbbing cock, as it repeatedly slapped against the side of the ottoman, as Chuck's talented tongue nearly had my body squirming right off the ottoman.

After Chuck was through rimming me he flipped me over on my back and put my legs on his shoulders. In less than a minute he greased up his cock and thrust it deep into my eager ass. I let out a loud moan and my body tensed-up as one of the cameramen filmed my facial expressions and squirming body movements, from a downward angle, while standing on a ladder.

No one yelled cut as I got closer and closer to cumming. This was the big moment. As my body tensed-up, I moaned loudly, gritting my teeth and started to shoot a huge load of warm, sticky cum all over my chest and face. When my cock was spent my body started to relax and I looked up at Chuck, he was smiling. He was pleased and that was all that mattered to me at the time.

After Chuck reviewed the film he seemed very satisfied with my performance. "Babe, you were off the charts. Keeping you hornier than hell really paid off big time."

The main film work was done and Chuck and checked into one of the bedrooms to rest for an hour. After standing under all those hot lights, having to start and stop scenes several times, being expected to get a hard-on on command and putting up with the cameramen grabbing my cock and ass when Chuck was not in the room, it felt really good to cuddle up naked next to my lover and get some needed rest.

One the ride home Chuck said that he was very proud of the way that I performed today. In his opinion, I was a natural. He was sure that in the next four scenes of the movie, I would do just as good. Chuck was starting me out in the business with my own movie. He is also going to use my interview film, the one that I did a beat off scene and ended up cumming without touching myself, as the introduction scene in the movie. That is how confident he is that the public will like me as much as he does and I don't intend to let him down.

After we had only gone a few blocks Chuck now handed me a photo album. "Look over these guys sweet cheeks." The first set of photos were of a red haired, super hung, smooth bodied, very muscular guy, who looked like he was in his early 20's. "Well Babe, I have interviewed all of these guys over the last two weeks. The red haired guy is Brad. He is 24, in very good shape and he has a ten-inch cock. He claimed that he can fuck all night. He's a real sex machine, but he is not very well educated. Personally, I don't think he even made it through high school. But, his brains are not what matters."

The second guy had dark hair, was semi-butch in appearance, with some chest hair and hair on his lower legs. He looked like he was in good shape and he was sporting a nice, fat 8 inch cock.

"That's Bill, he is 28 years old, a college graduate, nice personality and he loves to fuck."

The next stud was a boyish looking guy with a smooth bodied swimmer's body. He had about a 9-inch cock and a cute ass.

"That's Robert he is the same age as you, 19. He is a bottom, so you will be fucking him if you are in a scene with him. He is a mild mannered young man and a student at UCLA."

The last set of photos were of a supper hung, good-looking, very well built, light skinned black guy, who looked to be about 30 years old. My lover took a glance at the last guy and smiled, "That is Carlos. He is a 29-year-old Afro-Cuban, an Engineer by trade, very intelligent. He thinks his life is too dull at present and he wants to walk a little on the wild side for a change. The guy has a lot of class."

After I closed the book of photos my lover said, "Well Babe, pick out your next stud for scene two. I'll make the arrangements."

I just smiled, I must really be on a roll of good luck, my lover is a major porn stud, he owns the porn company that I am working for and I even get to pick the guy who gets to fuck me next. Man, I don't know what the future will bring but for now all I can say is I doubt that it will get any better. But, of course, being young and inexperienced, I just had to push my luck a little.

I looked at my lover, smiled and said, "Daddy can I have all of them, pleaseeee?"

My lover just started laughing, which I took as a good sign. "O.K. Babe, you got them. I'll hire them all for your picture."

He then gave me a more serious look. "Not that I am doing this because you are my lover and you are the best sex that I have ever had. It is a good business move to use fresh faces in a movie like this."

"Yes Daddy, you are right of course. You are the man. You are always right."

CHAPTER TWELVE

STRAIGHT GYM

The sun was just starting to go down when I finally made it to the gym after a hard day at school. My college course load this semester was starting to get really heavy and I needed to take a break from the academic grind. My way of relaxing is to get physical. Pumping iron really gets my blood flowing and helps to get the kinks out from all of that sitting in uncomfortable chairs for hours in boring classrooms.

As a gay male you would think that I would chose to go to a gym that has mostly a gay membership. It would not be hard to find such a gym in the Hollywood area of L.A., but I prefer to go to a nearby gym that is mostly straight.

I've been going to this mostly straight guy gym in the valley for the last two years. The membership is made up mostly of blue-collar types who work in the construction business.

Why would a good-looking, very muscular, young and hung gay guy want to lift weights with a bunch of straight dudes? Yes, I have heard all the stories. Straights are boring, uptight as hell, can be dangerous and they will not accept an openly gay guy in such a macho environment.

After going to the local, very straight gym for the last year, as an openly gay dude, I've had very little in the way of problems. O.K. there was that one mouthy guy who called me a fucking faggot and tried to push me against a locker, but a few fast moves soon had him crying in pain on the dressing room floor. He was rather civil to me after that.

After that incident, the guys at the gym soon learned that I was once an all-state high school wrestler and I am an ex-Navy Seal. It also, did not hurt to be 6'2" and 225 pounds of solid muscle. In short, I can lick almost all the guys in this gym, except maybe big Al the weight lifter and former pro-wrestler. But Al is a friendly guy and is no problem to me, thank God.

Going to a straight gym it has its pluses and minuses. On the plus side, I don't have a problem with guys always staring and hitting on me. If guys talk to me they usually just want to talk. At a straight gym guys actually go there to work out, not to find a date.

On the minus side, I have to watch myself; it is not polite to stare at people, especially in the shower room, even if they are a real hunk. I usually talk a shower alone, straight guys are still a little uptight about taking a shower with an openly gay guy, except the older men, they seem to not really care about such things. This situation is not really all that bad on my part, since I never could get use to the way straight guys take showers. Like, what is it with these straight guys always facing the shower room wall and not looking at other naked guys, talk about being uptight. Even this strange situation has an upside you do get to see some nice looking asses.

Yes, I know what you are going to want to know, are any of the dudes at my gym available for a little walk on the wild side? The answer is yes and no. Even if I disregard the small number of gay guys that I know at the gym, there are the fence jumpers.

The fence jumpers are the mostly straight guys that will approach a good-looking, straight acting gay guy like me for a little action. I mean action, as in a good blowjob, or a chance to fuck my pretty ass. Occasionally, some of these fence jumpers will surprise you and want a lot more than just a B.J., or a fuck.

Since straight guys are eager to get a good blowjob from a pro and turning them down can be a big pain in the ass, I let it be known through the gym grapevine, or through personal encounters, that I had certain standards. If a guy wanted some action from me he had to be on my type and meet certain standards.

Why standards, well it is a way of getting rid of the non-serious types. It is a pay your own way type of system that will scare away most of the straights who just want a freebee.

My standards were rather simply, if you were my type and you wanted a good blowjob you had to make out with me first. If you wanted to fuck my pretty ass you had to eat my ass first. These rules help a great deal to get rid of all but the serious prospects. Did these rules leave anyone standing, hell yes!

This game can be a lot like fishing. I will get a fair number of prospects that you that are not my type, who I will politely throw back in the water, but some of the people who approached me were a real surprise. Some prospects were people who I would never had expected to approach me, so much for the gaydar thing.

The first interesting guy to hit the bait was Carlos. Carlos is a dark haired guy, in his early 20's. He is the type of person who does not say much and he would not even get noticed if it wasn't for the fact that he is a very good-looking young man. I had not paid much attention to him. He was the type of guy that if you make eye contact with him he will act like he doesn't like you and looks away.

Late one night I was taking a shower alone, not many people were in the gym, when Carlos came in and started to take a shower right next to me. This way very non-straight guy type of behavior and my gaydar started to ring off the hock. Carlos turned on the shower and got completely wet and then said, "Hey Randy, I heard that you give great head if a guy is willing to make out with you."

I was a little startled that such a shy person like Carlos was hitting on me, but I looked down and saw that his big cock was already half hard. He was not joking.

I quickly decided to test how serious he was. Without saying a word I took the bar of soap that I was using and I walked up to Carlos and I started to soap down his back as I looked into his big puppy dog eyes. He didn't bat an eyelash, a good sign that he was serious. Without saying a word I just started to kiss his willing lips as I dropped the soap and ran my hands down his back until I had a good, two handed hold on his ass cheeks.

Now he began to surprise me. He started to lead rather than to follow. His lips moved over to my ear lobes and he started to lick and kiss his way down the side of my neck. He was starting to get me hot and my stiff cock was rubbing against his. I grabbed the back of his head and pulled it back exposing his lips so that I could start kissing him again. I squeezed his ass cheeks really hard as our tongues played tag with each other and my stiff cock rubbed against his.

After only a few minutes of making out and rubbing my hands all over his soapy back and ass I knew I just had to have it. I turned Carlos around so that his soapy backside was in the shower and I licked my way down his chest and stomach until I was licking his big, firm balls. He started to moan and his body shook.

"God, that feels soooo… good!"

As I slowly worked my way up his big throbbing cock and my tongue started to lick the head of his dick, he put both of his hands on the back of my head and shoved his cock deep into my mouth.

"Suck it, please suck it good!"

As I deep throated his cock repeatedly, Carlos rapidly started to build up to climax. Suddenly, his big cock started to swell.

"Oh God, Ohhh...!"

As Carlos shoot a big load of warm, sweet cum down my eager throat I gave my throbbing hard cock a few fast strokes and shot my load all over myself.

As Carlos's cock stated to soften I licked the remaining cum off his cock as his body mildly shook. As Carlos's cock slipped out of my mouth he kneeled down and gave me a long and deep kiss.

"Man, you are a great cock sucker. Thank you, I wanted my first time to be with an expert like you."

He kissed me one more time and then he walked out of the shower room. With the warm shower water bathing my folded knees I just relaxed for a moment and started to smile. Man, I just gave a virgin his first blowjob.

The second unexpected straight guy to hit on me was Frank. Frank is a plain looking, extremely muscular, construction worker, with short military like brown hair. He is in his late 20's and up to quite recently I thought that he was completely straight. Well, it seems he is not as completely as he appeared.

Frank had always been friendly to me and had even given me some pointers on weight training, but in reality I had very little contact with him in the two years that I have been going to this gym. Than one afternoon, while I was drinking a protein drink, just after my workout, he walked up to me with a slight smile on his face.

"Hey Randy, I haven't seen you in months."

He slapped me on the back and then squeezed my shoulder really hard.

"Well Frank, you been doing alright?"

"Well sort of, but I want to talk to you about something."

"What is it?"

He swallowed hard and said, "I was just thinking that maybe you could help me out with something?"

"What is it Frank, just name it."

"Well, I have a temporary women problem. My women in going to be back East for a month and you know me I like to fuck at least twice a week."

He was silent for a moment and he looked a little embarrassed. "Well, I have heard that you will let a guy ride your pretty ass if he is willing to eat it first."

"Yes, that is true, are you up to it Frank."

He now smiled. "As long as no one knows about it, I have no problem with it. I eat my women's ass all the time and you have a nice hairless ass just like her. So, can I get a chance to ride your ass?"

My cock was already starting to get hard just thinking about this rugged stud plowing my eager ass.

"O.K., are you busy later tonight."

"Hell, I'm ready to go right now."

It only took us about 20 minutes to drive to my house. As we walked up the stairs I felt Frank's hand grab my ass and squeeze really hard. He was an eager top.

After unlocking the front door I led Frank into my bedroom and we both quickly undressed. I threw back the covers on my bed and piled two pillows on top of each other in the middle. As I laid face down on the bed with the pillows under my hips I looked back at Frank standing next to the bed. He was staring at my pretty ass and smiling as his big cock throbbed up and down. He was more than ready.

As Frank got on the bed behind and his hands parted my ass cheeks I laid my head down on the mattress. The feel of a warm, wet tongue on my asshole caused my upper body to tense up and slightly lift off the mattress. What followed what 15 minutes of expert rimming that soon had me moaning and squirming. Man, he was good at eating ass.

When I was ready to have my ass plowed I stopped Frank and gave him some Lube and a rubber. Frank looked very eager and He slowly entered me and with each stroke shoved his big cock in deeper and deeper, until he was fucking me long and hard. The man was really horny, he shot his load in only a few minutes, but he did not stop. Frank fucked me for the next hour or so and he shot off at least another two times before he seemed satisfied. As frank's cock slid out of my ass frank slapped my bare ass a few times.

"Man, you have a great fucking ass we have to do this again some time."

After we took a shower, I soaped down his body and he soaped down mine, I gave him my phone number. As he left I said to myself, "I hope he phones. That man can sure eat ass and fuck like a pro. Who cares if he won't kiss me, he can ride my ass anytime."

The next straight guy story is about Brad. Brad is not someone that I at first noticed when I first started to go to my gym. He was probably 17 years old at the time. He didn't even show up on my gaydar.

After he became 18 and started to go to the same college as me, as well as the same gym, I noticed that he would stare at me at times from a distance. But, I can't say that he really interested me. I never actually thought much about him.

Brad is a blond young man, more cute than pretty or handsome. The features that make Brad's face stand out are his big lips and nice smile. In the two years he has been going to the gym he has made a great deal of progress. He has added quite a lot of well-defined muscle to his frame. It was just recently that I took notice of him. Not just because of the fact that he has been staring at me at times for the last two years, but because his body has become more man like and he has started to actually talk to me in a social manner. He has started to ask me for some tips on how to do certain exercises.

Up until just recently, I thought he was just another straight young man who wanted a body like mine. Actually, I was soon to find out, he wanted to more than just look at my body. One afternoon, while I was doing sets of arm curls, Brad walked up to me and asked if he could talk to me in private. He looked a little nervous. I just nodded my head and motioned for him to follow me to a vacate area of the gym.

"What is it Brad?"

Brad looked at the floor for a moment, he acted very nervous.

"Well, I... want to know if I am sexy enough....well, enough to get some action with you."

The whole time that he was talking he was looking at the floor and not me. I reached out, put my hand under his chin, and lifted his head up so that he was now facing me.

"Yes, you are sexy enough and if you want some action you've got it." He smiled ear to ear. "Really?"

"Yes, when do you want to come over to my place?"

"Anytime man, anytime you want."

After finishing our workout routines Brad followed me over to my house. As we entered the front door I told Brad to make himself comfortable I had to check my e-mail. When I walked back into the living room Brad was sitting buck-naked in one of the high back chairs stroking his big stiff cock. He stared at me with a broad smile on his face. He was ready, very ready.

I decided to give Brad a little show and I started to do a slow striptease. As I took off my shirt I rubbed my hands all over my upper body as Brad's eyes got bigger and bigger, as he continued to stroke his big, stiff cock. By the time I had stripped off all of my clothes Brad was sitting in the chair, eyed wide open, with his stiff cock pulsating up and down on his stomach.

Now something totally unexpected happened. This cute, inexperienced, straight boy, got down on his knees, put his hands behind his back, bowed his head and said, "Sir, please teach me how to please you."

I was a little startled, but I know how to play this game.

"So, you want to play slave games, do you boy?"

"Yes Sir, I want you to train me to serve."

I reached down and played with the hair on his head, before I proceeded to run my hand down his back and played with his ass. He reacted like a puppy being petted. This boy was a real surprise and I was going to find out if he was just playing around or was he serious.

"So boy, you want some training in how to serve, do you?"

"Yes Sir, I want to be trained to serve you Sir!"

I had a feeling about this. He seems to have more knowledge about this game than if he had just read a book. I was going to find out what he was all about.

"Stand up for inspection Boy!"

"Yes Sir!"

As he stood up he assumed a submissive posture, with his hands behind his back and his head bowed. As I started my inspection of his naked body his stiff cock just throbbed up and down. He was enjoying this. I inspected his neck and proceeded down his body until I ran my hands over his feet. He had an almost perfect, well-developed, muscular, very well defined body. His body was almost hairless, with only a little hair under his arms and on his crotch. His complexion was flawless. All of this was accented by a stiff and throbbing, fat, 8-inch cock and firm hairless balls.

"O.K. Boy, now spread your feet about two feet apart and bend over."

"Yes Sir!"

I slapped his bare ass a few times and then I bent down behind him and spread his ass cheeks. The boy had a beautiful pink asshole and I quickly ran my fingers over the crack of his ass and starting to play with his asshole. His body tensed up and he moaned a little.

"Well Boy, have you ever been fucked before?"

"No Sir, I want you to be the first to fuck me."

This answer startled me.

"Boy, have you ever sucked a cock or had your cock sucked?"

"Sir, I have sucked cock many times and I have had my cock sucked."

I smiled a little, at least he had some experience. "But Sir, I am willing to be trained to do anything that you want me too."

This horny boy had only limited sexual experience. It sounds like he has been playing with his friends or hanging around some glory holes place. All he knows at present is how to suck cock. Maybe, this whole scene was starting to bring some sort of teacher instinct out of me, because I was starting to really be turned on by the prospect of training my own semi-virgin, daddy's boy.

After inspecting Brad's pretty ass I got up and sat down in a chair, leaned back and then ordered Brad to get on his knees in front of the chair.

"O.K. Boy let's start your training with something that you know how to do, start licking my balls boy."

"Yes Sir!"

The feel of his hot, wet tongue on my balls caused my body to tense up as I slowly stroked my own cock. After only a few minutes I ordered Brad to get my cock wet and to start sucking it. He smiled as he was licking my cock. I also noticed that his stiff cock was wildly throbbing up and down, like an animal in heat. He was really enjoying this whole scene.

After enjoying a rather good blowjob for about 10 minutes I decided that it was time to deflower this virgin. I pulled Brad's head off of my cock, he looked a little disappointed, and I bent down and kissed him for several minutes as I played with one of his nipples. He moaned and squirmed a little.

I now walked over to the sofa and grabbed a pillow and through it on the floor. "O.K. Boy lay face down on the floor with the pillow under your hips."

"Yes Sir!"

As brad did as he was ordered I got a towel, a jar of lube and some condoms from my bedroom.

As I walked back into the front room I looked at Brad lying face down on the pillow. He was smiling at me. "Boy I am going to rim your pretty ass and then I am going to fuck you. Do you have any problems with that?"

"No Sir, none at all. My ass is yours Sir!"

I parted his ass cheeks and started to tongue his pretty pink asshole. His body began to shake and he moaned. As the minutes pasted, he put on quite a show as he squirmed and moaned, as his body repeatedly tensed up. When I was done rimming his pretty, rounded ass, I stood up on my knees and started to put and grease down my condom with one hand as my other hand shoved grease up the Brad's ass. He moaned and started to move his ass up and down as my fingers lubed the inside of his ass. I withdraw my fingers and he then looked back at me and smiled. This boy wants to be fucked, he wants it really bad.

I leaned forward and put the head of my dick on Brad's asshole. As I slowly pushed the head of my cock into his ass he moaned just a little. My cock slid deep into his ass without any trouble and I started to take long, slow strokes, until his ass loosened up and then I started to really shove it to him. He just moaned and moved his ass up and down with the motion of my thrusts.

"Fuck me Daddy, fuck me good."

He was enjoying this as much as I was. His ass was nice and firm. It was like fucking to firm, warm and moist, velvet pillows. Man, this boy has a great fucking ass.

With each thrust the boy squirmed more and moaned louder, which only made my dick harder and harder. Finally, after about a half hour of great fucking I withdraw my cock and shoot my loud on Brad's back.

Now I stood up, leaned over, and grabbed Brad by the hair on the back of his head. "Get up Boy!"

"Yes Sir!"

When Brad was on his feet I notice that he had cum all over the sofa pillow. He had really enjoyed his first fucking. I gave him a long deep kiss as I played with his still firm balls.

"Well Boy, it's time for a shower. Your first training session is over."

"Thank you Sir, I will look forward to my next training session with you."

What happened next? Well, I've stopped trying to predict what straight boys will do. I just go with the flow now. As for Carlos, Frank and Brad, well Carlos got married recently, it seems he found a girl who sucks cock as well as I do. Frank's women came back from her trip and I guess he is rimming her again. Well Brad, he is a completely different story. He is now living with me and he has developed into the best-trained, most devoted Daddy's Boy in L.A.

CHAPTER THIRTEEN

MIKE RETURNS

As my master's property my life had become very simple, my mind and life were completely focused on serving and pleasing my master, nothing else mattered. The concerns of the outside world had disappeared. I no longer worried about a career, schooling, taxes and any type of news. These things did not apply to my life they were the concerns of my master. If my master thought that I needed to know something he would tell me about it. My world had become very small, predictable and safe. My world consisted of only two people, myself and my master, but my ideal life was about to change.

One day, after my master had left to go to town on business, I heard a knock on the front door. Before I opened the door, I looked through a window to see who it was. When I saw that it was my old, kinky best friend Mike, I smiled a little, before I opened the door.

As I opened the door Mike looked a little startled, as he looked over my muscular, well-defined, hairless, naked body, from one end to the other. "Wow, your man sure has put a lot of work into you!" I smiled and asked Mike to come in.

I put my arms around Mike and said, "It's good to see you again." As I let go of Mike and backed away he did not say a thing, his eyes continued to inspect my naked body. "Mike, are you all right?" He now looked directly at me and smiled, "Yes I'm all right I just can't get over how great you look. You have made a lot of changes in yourself."

"No not really, my master made the changes in me."

"He sure knows what he is doing. Your master has not only really built you up he has even made your cock a lot bigger than I remember."

"No, it is not bigger. It just looks bigger since my body hair was permanently shaved off."

I asked Mike to sit down in one of the armchairs in the living room, as I sat on my knees in front of him. I am not allowed to sit on the chairs without my master's permission. As I looked at Mike he seemed a little nervous, as if he had something on his mind that he didn't know how to handle. I know Mike he had something on his mind, but I didn't worry about what it was, Mike would give up his secret. Mike could never keep a secret for very long.

"Well Mike, what have you done since college?"

"Nothing that really matters, I left college after you did. It wasn't any fun without you to pal around with and I spent a year in Chicago trying to figure out what to do with myself."

"Don't small talk me Mike, you have something important on your mind, what is it?" Mike looked down at the floor for a half smile and looked at me. "Well Randy, I don't know how you will take this, but frankly, when it comes to what I would really like to do with my life, I would like to be just like you."

Mike's comment did not startle me in the least. I knew Mike, like he was my twin brother. "Yes, I had a feeling that you were thinking like that, from the time that you saw me with my master in town over a year ago. I could see a hint of envy in your eyes."

"Damn right, more than just envy, I had to go home and beat-off twice, I was so turned-on."

"So Randy, you can figure out what I want, I want what you have, to be the property of your stud master. Do you think that you can help me out and maybe get me an interview or something with your master?" As I looked into Mike's eyes, I could see that he was completely serious about being trained to serve.

At this point, I got up and walked into the kitchen, leaving Mike sitting silently. I looked out the kitchen window and tried to figure out how to answer Mike's question. I had never asked my master for anything. But, I did owe Mike a lot.

As I walked back into the living room, Mike was still sitting silently in the armchair, with his head bowed, with a tense, lost look on his face. When I knelt down on the floor in front of Mike, his head rose and he looked at me. "You know that if my master likes the idea of training you Mike, that you won't be playing a kids game." Mike nodded in agreement. "If my master goes for it, you will have two months to impress him, before he will offer to let you sign papers."

"That's O.K., I'll work hard and I will do anything to please him."

"Now Mike, let's talk serious, if you get the chance to sign papers, you are owed for life and you can be sold at any time, for any reason."

"Yes, I'm like you Randy, I was born to serve a man. The idea of being completely owned by a man and existing only to please him, sounds like heaven to me."

"Mike you haven't changed a bit. You still think with your dick and if an idea makes your dick hard, that's what you are going to do. But I must say that this time your dick probably knows what is best for you." Mike just looked at me and smiled. "The idea of being trained and owned by your master, not only gets my dick hard, it almost give me a heart attack. But, that is not the reason I am here today. I have given this idea a lot of serious thought and I know I'm exactly like you Randy, I was born to serve a master."

"Okay, for the sake of our friendship and your dick, I will ask my master to interview you as a training prospect. But, no guarantees and you have to help me put the hay away in the barn today." Mike smiled and then almost bolted out of the chair. "Well, it's a deal, now let's get to work."

It was almost sundown, when my master returned from town. Mike and I were just getting to the end of our hay-moving job. I quickly took off my work boots and overalls and started to walk naked over to greet my master. I knelt in front of him and asked permission to speak.

"Speak Boy."

"Sir, an old friend from college came by today to ask for my help." There was a moment of silence.

"What type of help did he need from you, Boy?"

"Sir, he wanted my help in getting a trainee interview with you."

"So, your friend wants me to train him to serve?"

"Yes Sir, he is very eager."

"Who is this friend of yours, have I ever met him?"

"Yes Sir, I introduced you to Mike when we were in town to get supplies over a year ago."

"Yes, I remember him, a fairly good looking, dark haired boy, that you said had a really big dick."

"Yes Sir, 12 inches."

"He may well be a good prospect, but I can't tell until I talk to him and inspect his body. Where is he right now?"

"Sir, he's in the barn, he has been helping me with the hay."

"Good, go back to the barn and get him ready for an interview. Have him stripped and kneeling on the living room carpet, in 20 minutes."

"Yes Sir!"

"And, one more thing Boy, if he turns out to be a waste of my time, you are going to be hurting tonight."

"Yes Sir, I understand."

As I walked back to the barn, I could feel the tension rising in my body. I had never taken a risk like this, it was a gamble. When I got to the barn, Mike was still piling bales of hay in the back. When he noticed me, he just looked at me and didn't say a thing. I smiled and said, "Well Mike, get naked, your interview starts in 15 minutes." Mike was eager to please all right, before I finished, he was starting to get undressed. In only about a minute he was standing in front of me buck naked, with a throbbing hard-on.

After discussing a few do's and don'ts, most of which Mike already knew, I told him to follow me to the house. On the way I couldn't help but think, what if Mike blows it, my backside will be getting a good belting tonight.

As we entered the living room, I closed the door behind us and told Mike to kneel on the carpet, put his arms behind his back and bow his head. I kneeled down next to him and we waited. After a few short minutes, my master entered the room, wearing only his boxer shorts and he walked over and stood in front of us. "Boy, is this your friend?"

"Yes Sir, this is Mike."

"Well Mike, I am going to ask you some questions. I want truthful, adult answers, no kids' stuff. Do you understand, Boy?"

"Yes Sir, I understand."

"Mike, my first question is why do you want me to train you to serve?"

"Sir, because I know you are the best and I know that I was born to serve."

"Mike, do you have any experience in serving a master?"

"Yes Sir, about a years' worth in Chicago."

"Why are you not still with your master?"

"Sir, he was not right for me, he was too soft. I needed a stricter master, one who will fully train and develop me, Sir!"

"Mike, what if I trained you and then decided to sell you to another master, how do you feel about that?"

"Sir, I wouldn't have any feelings about being sold. I would be my master's property. If he decided to sell me, he has the right to do so, I would not complain, at all."

Mike's answers seemed to please my master. Hell, even I thought that they sounded good. It seems, Mike was telling me the truth, when he said that he has given this matter a lot of thought.

My master ordered Mike to get on his feet. Mike quickly stood up and assumed a submissive posture. I was ordered to get up and go sit against a wall and just watch. Mike was really enjoying this scene his cock was already hard and throbbing. As my master inspected Mike's naked body, starting with his head and working his way down, he would occasionally twist his nipples, squeeze his balls, or slap his bare ass really hard. My master wanted to see how Mike responded to pain. From my past experience, I knew that Mike would pass this test. Pain just turns Mike on.

After finishing with the first part of his inspection, my master turned and walked into the kitchen, leaving Mike standing with his hands behind his back and his head bowed. Mike stood silently and didn't move an inch. I half smiled, as I watched Mike's big cock throb slowly up and down. When my master returned, he had a jar and a towel with him.

"All right Mike, bend over the back of the couch and spread your feet about three feet apart."

"Yes Sir!" After Mike obeyed his order, my master knelt behind him, greased up several fingers, spread Mike's ass cheeks and started to probe his anus first, with one finger, than two, than three. As my master probed deeper and deeper with his fingers, Mike began to moan and squirm. When my master shoved his whole greased hand into Mike's anus he started to shake and moan louder, as my master started to move his fist around inside of him.

Just when Mike was starting to act as if he was getting close to cumming, my master squeezed the head of his big dick, to keep him from cumming, as he withdrew his fist. Mike's body relaxed and Mike's face had a sign of relief on it, like he had almost lost his load.

My master, now stood up, cleaned his hand with the towel and ordered Mike to get on his knees. Mike quickly obeyed, as my master dropped his boxer shorts, exposing his big, hard, throbbing cock. Watching my master inspect Mike was beginning to get to me; my mouth was starting to water, as I mentally started to beg for a chance to replace Mike's mouth with my own.

As my master stood in front of Mike he ordered him to eat and lick his balls. Mike's head sprang forward and he buried his face in my master's balls, as his big cock pulsated, up and down, like a horny dog. To Mike, this moment must have been like he died and went to heaven. He had lusted for a chance like this since we were both in college.

As my master began to moan approvingly of Mike's efforts, he leaned down, grabbed Mike by the back of his head, and pulled his head back. "All right Mike, it's time to find out if you can suck dick."

"Get it wet!"

"Yes Sir!" After mike had licked every inch of my master's cock, he was given the order that he had wanted to hear for over a year. "Now Mike, suck it and suck it good."

"Yes Sir!" Mike didn't need any more encouragement, he deep throated my master's big cock, clean down to his public hair, in one motion.

As my master enjoyed Mike's cock sucking technique, I sat on the floor, with my back against the wall, with a roaring hard-on, visualizing over and over again, the pleasure of sucking my master's cock. I had always eagerly sucked my master's cock, praying for the moment when he would start to moan and tense up, just before he was about to shoot a heavy load of sweet cum down my thirsty throat.

By the time I was finished with my envious daydreaming, mike was already using his tongue to clean my master's cock of the last drops of cum. My master smiled, he looked pleased. I smiled a little. Since my master was pleased, I was pleased.

My master looked down at Mike and smiled, "Not bad, not bad."

"On your feet and follow me up the stairs." As Mike sprang to his feet, he almost shouted, "Yes Sir!"

After my master and Mike disappeared up the stairs to my master's bedroom, I sat on the floor, slowly pumping my throbbing cock and quietly listening for the sounds from upstairs that I knew would come.

After only a few minutes of silence, I started to hear the sounds of squeaking bedsprings and soft moaning, that grew louder and louder, over the next half hour. I smiled, as I pumped my cock a little faster, as I listened to the sounds of my master royally fucking Mike's ass.

Over the next year, it was interesting to watch Mike go through the different stages of the same training program, that had completely changed me from a kinky, college pretty boy, into a well-disciplined man slave. At first Mike, was subject to a very intense and strict training program, which is a lot like a military boot camp, just before he was run through the mental part of the training.

My master calls the mental stage of his training program, the Mental Psychoactive Restructuring Stage. This is the stage that works with a prospects sub-conscious mind. It uses the sub-conscious mind to help the trainee to focus completely on only one subject, how to serve and please his master. This is the stage that my master is really state of the art. He developed the whole program himself.

The system is not full proof. It won't always work. The person must be a willing subject, with the natural ability to make such a change. My master has perfected this program. He has found that he can take a naturally submissive gay make and train him to be an extremely disciplined and eager to serve man slave. I am the first example of how well the system works.

Over the next year, Mike's body changed, from a boy's body to a muscular, well-defined man's body. My master's training program added 25 pounds of muscle to Mike's frame. It was at this point that Mike's body hair was permanently shaved off, which made his big cock look even bigger. Now physically, Mike looked a lot like me.

Mentally, Mike changed from a happy go lucky young man, who acted more like a teenager, into a very disciplined and focused man slave. Mike had become a total slave, who lived for the pleasure of serving his master. Now Mike, is not just my kinky friend from my high school and college days, he is my slave brother.

The addition of Mike as my slave brother has been a big help in running the ranch. Now, the jobs around the ranch get done faster and we have been able to add a few new projects.

Adding Mike to the household has also improved the quality of our master's life. He now has two hot, young, stud slaves to keep care of his needs, or the needs of any houseguests that he may invite to spend some time at the ranch.

My master is making important friends in the national and international leather community. He has also, made some very important connections with some government people in Washington D.C., he says that it is part of his project. I don't know what that means he has never explained what the project is to me.

At least once a month, we will have houseguests at the ranch. They are usually masters and their slaves that my master knows from his leather community connections. These guests are always physically in great shape, my master has a thing about physical fitness, so any master or slave who does not have the self-discipline to keep care of their bodies, will not be invited to my master's ranch.

The master's and slaves that meet my master's standards, regardless of age, are always in good physical shape. When my master has guests, they are given the opportunity to pick either Mike or I, to entertain them in any way that they want. Mike and I look forward to having houseguests it gives us the opportunity to explore new ways of pleasing a master.

Most houseguests just use us for sex. We sexually please them and sleep with them. In some cases we are ordered to put on a little live sex show. My master has found that some of his houseguests enjoy seeing me lay face down, on the living room floor, with several pillows under my waist, while they watch me squirm as Mikes eats my ass and then proceeds to make me loudly moan and sometimes violently shake, as he fucks me, long and hard, with his huge cock.

Other guests are more interested in pain than sex. Such guest will pick one of us to take out to the barn, to be used as a torture subject. I usually get picked for this duty. It seems such masters get a great deal of pleasure, out of watching a blond, hung, well-built, pretty boy like me, tensing, squirming, crying and sometimes screaming in acute pain, as they slowly and skillfully push me toward my limits to tolerating pain.

I was very pleased with having my master all to myself for the first year of my slavery, but I must admit that the addition of Mike and the challenge of pleasing my master's house guests, has changed my life for the better. But at times, I must admit, I do miss that first year.

CHAPTER FOURTEEN

THE AUCTION

The trip by car to the site of the auction took 6 hours. The auction was to be held at a former French air base in an isolated area of Morocco. Driving up to the main building for the event we could see at least a dozen private jets on the airfield runway. The event parking lot was beginning to fill up.

We had arrived two hours before the pre-show and my master decided that I should rest before the show. My master found me a bed in a small room in one of the buildings at the auction site. He wanted me to get a little sleep before I was to be put on display. My master wanted me to look refreshed when I stood naked on the display platform during the pre-show. He told me to try to get some sleep and he would be back for me in about an hour and a half. I took off my cotton robe and sandals and crawled naked into bed.

I managed to relax but it was hard for me to get to sleep. My body was tense. The reality of the day was beginning to cause my sexual energy level to rise. The thought that in just a few hours I was to be standing naked on an auction block, in front of several hundred men, ready to be sold to the highest bidder had caused my cock to get throbbing hard and I found it hard to get any sleep.

As I tried to get some sleep my mind drifted back to the day, one year ago, that radically changed my life. It was the day that my lover Carlos sold me to the slavers.

We had gone on vacation to visit Carlos's native country Morocco. Everything was right and proper about the trip. Carlos seemed very happy to be visiting Morocco again.

Than it happen. While walking back to our hotel after having dinner, a van pulled up and blocked our path. Three men got out and grabbed me. My lover did nothing. He just stood there with his arms folded across his chest.

The men forced a ball gag into my mouth and handcuffed my arms behind my back. As I was thrown into the van I could see my lover standing on the sidewalk expressing no emotions at all.

I fought my captors at first, but then one of them told me that if I did not agree to be trained and sold as a slave, I would be sold for slaughter to a torture master. My death would be very painful.

I was relieved to hear the footsteps of my master returning. I hadn't been able to sleep I was only able to close my eyes and rest. My body was tense and my cock was still hard. My master ordered me to get up and to follow him. I quickly obeyed and I was soon following my master naked down a long hallway to what turned out to be a large, two-story room. I was led to a small round platform that stood about one foot off the floor. The small platform was surrounded by a temporary rope barrier that stood about three feet tall. My master told me to mount the platform. After I got on the small platform I was ordered to stand with my feet about two feet apart. My master than shackled my ankles to the platform.

My master now put my auction number chain around my neck. I was to be number 17. He then gave me my orders, "Boy this is the pre-show. You will stand on this platform, with your hands at your side and look directly forward. During the next two hours potential buyers will review the slaves to be sold tonight. If a possible buyer is interested in a closer review of your body the attendant that is assigned to you will let him do a physical inspection. This pre-show is designed to give potential buyers a better idea of which slaves they will want to bid on at the auction tonight. Do you understand Boy?"

"Yes Sir!"

My master turned me over to the attendant who was assigned to look after me and then he left. My master was to be the auctioneer tonight and he had to get his staff ready for the show. I felt a certain amount of pride in the fact that my own master was the one who was going to sell me tonight.

I stood naked on my platform with a throbbing hard on, as the other slaves were shackled to their platforms. Over all, about 20 slaves were put on display. Since I was on the outer edge of the room I was able to see all of the slaves that were to be sold. The slaves on display were a mixed group of ages and races. They ranged from very boyish pretty boys to very rugged looking, semi hairy men. The one that looked the oldest, an Asian slave, was about in his late 20's and the youngest, a blond smooth bodied, pretty boy could not have been older than about 18. I was happy to see that none of them could match my muscular and well-define body or my big dick. I smiled, I wanted very badly to score the highest price tonight and make my master proud of me.

After waiting only about 15 minutes the potential buyers came into the hall. The men were all dressed casually and they walked among the slaves to be sold, looking over each one and sometimes writing notes down on each slave. I was surprised to see that some of the potential buyers had brought along their personal slaves. The slaves were naked just like me, but with a small difference, they had red slave collars, not black like the slaves to be sold tonight. A crowd soon formed around me and my attendant started to get requests to physically inspect my naked body. The first person to inspect me was young looking man that looked like he was in his early 30's. He had a very stern look in his eyes and he was all business. He inspected me just like a rancher would inspect a prized stallion that he was interested in buying. He smiled a bit after he was though as he wrote down a few notes on his pre-show form.

Having one after the other of the buyer's man handle my naked body was something that really turned me on. It kept my cock throbbing hard during the hours of the pre-show. My master had trained me in what to expect at this auction. Only one unexpected event happened that caught me by surprise. It did not startle me it just made me smile a little. It concerned a slave that one of the buyers had bought to the show. He was a good-looking, dark haired, nicely hung slave in his mid-twenties. It seems that I had quiet an effect on his cock. He stood in front of me, on the other side of the rope barrier, just staring directly at me while he licked his lips and his hard cock just throbbed wildly up and down like he was a dog in heat. I wondered if his master would take note that his slave thought that I was really hot.

Before the pre-show was over I had been physically inspected by almost a hundred men. My naked and aroused body had been caressed, fondled, tickled, slapped, grabbed and probed. Over 30 men had inspected my asshole with their greased fingers and in some cases their whole hand. Two of the men actually recognized me as a well-known porn star. It was a fact that seemed to impress them. As the crowd left the hall I could not help but smile. I had been the main attraction of the pre-show and that should guarantee that I will bring a high price at the auction tonight.

After the pre-show was over and the hall had been cleared of the potential buyers my master unshackled me from the platform. As I stepped down to the floor my master grabbed my balls and lightly squeezed them. My body tensed up. "Boy you did very well. The buyers paid a lot of attention to you." He smiled and released my balls. "It is going to be really interesting to see what price you bring at the auction tonight."

It would be another five hours before the auction was to begin and my master wanted me primed and ready. After taking a shower my master and I had some dinner before I was to be taken me over to the auction hall for a little rehearsal.

During dinner my master decided that it was the right time to tell me what it was all about. That is the system that I was now part of. "Boy, this system was developed about 8 years ago to fill a need. To fill a need is the reason most new business concepts come into existence. The need was to supply well-trained man slaves to rich, over worked, gay business executives, who were into the leather scene."

"The master who buys the slave gets a good-looking, well trained man slave, for a price of between $200,000 to possibly one million dollars. For most of our clients the cost of a fine man slave is no more than pocket change to them.

My clients think of this arrangement in a business sense. If a master buys a slave like you for let's say $400,000. If just figure that cost over a ten year period, it comes out to $40,000 a year. That is far less than what a rich man would pay to hire an experienced servant.

Add to these figures the fact that the slave can be resold. The figure of $40,000 a year will drop considerably and it is possible that the buyer of said slave could actually earn a profit.

"The slave that our clients buy will take care of their house and their cocks better than any lover or sugar boy would. The master never has to buy the slave a new car or take him to Europe and best of all he never has to argue with them about anything. A slave is the best servant a rich gay man could have and for no more than a well-trained valet would cost and the valet would not suck his cock or sleep with him."

"The masters here tonight have had a good year financially and I believe that I can sell you for about a million dollars. You are top quality and the clients that we deal with really like quality."

As I sat naked with a throbbing hard on just across the table from my master I found it hard to believe that anyone was going to pay a million dollars to have me suck their cocks and sleep with them. I was just a good-looking mass of raging hormones, who was use to thinking more with his big cock than his head. Why anyone would pay a small fortune to use me as their sex slave was hard for me to understand.

But, due mostly to my training, I had adjusted extremely well to my new station in life. I am a slave and my life is serving my master. I no longer have a desire to rejoin the world of so-called free people.

The auction hall was an old airplane hangar not too far from the room that was used for the pre-show. My master had me put on a pair of sandals so that I could walk on the hot asphalt of the airfield runway. I walked behind my master with beads of sweat running down my naked body. Several of the potential buyers saw us and they stopped what they were doing and just stared at my naked body.

The airplane hangar had been made ready for the auction. It had a large stage, with curtains and a long runway that extended halfway into the audience section. The room must have contained at least 200 seats, arranged in rows of ten.

My master led me backstage and he showed me the little room where I would wait for my turn on the stage. The room was small, with only enough room for a cot like bed and a lamp. The room door was marked with my auction number, number 17.

My master now led me though the routine that I was to follow. My number would be coming up and the hall attendant would knock on the door of my room and tell me that I had 3 minutes. During these 3 minutes I was to put on my number chain, compose myself and walk out to stand behind the curtain and wait for my number to be called. When I hear my number I was to walk out on the runway and mount the auction platform at the end of the runway. At this point my master would introduce me and point out my best points as the auction platform slowly rotated. After my introduction and review my master wanted my cock to perform. When I was asked to I was to mentally cause my cock to shot a big load. After I had shot my load the bidding would begin.

After I was sold I was to walk down a section of stairs to the right of the auction platform and an attendant would take me to a holding room. My new master would claim me as his new property after the auction was over and payment had been made.

The next half hour my master walked through what I was to do tonight, I sat in my small room and waited for my number to be called and then I waited behind the curtain before I heard my number and then I walked out on the runway and mounted the platform. My master went over his introduction and pointed out my best points. The whole rehearsal felt so real that my cock wildly throbbed up and down. If my master had ordered me to cum I could have gotten off in less than half a minute.

After putting me though my paces at the auction hall my master returned me to my small room. My master gave me a glass of water with some herbal exacts in it, they were designed to make me super horny in order to guarantee that I would be able to cum without touching myself at the right moment. I drank the water and my master told me to get some sleep. My master now left to run the other slaves though the same rehearsal that I had just been though. It seems that my master gave me special consideration when he ran me though what I had to do. I smiled and drifted off to sleep.

When the time of the auction was approaching my master woke me up and had me put on only a pair of sandals, before I followed my master over to the auction hall. The slaves and the potential buyers were already filing into the airfield hanger. My master led me to my waiting room and told me to sit down on the cot and get my mind in focus I had about 20 minutes before the auction began. My number was 17, but I would be the fifth slave to be on stage tonight.

I could not get any rest, the herbal drink and the fact that I had not been allowed to cum in nearly a month had me so horny that my cock was hard as a rock. I sat on my cot, with my back against the wall started to think about what was about to happen to me for the next five years. Would he be a good master or would he be a cruel master? I did not know, but instead of being scared, as I expected, I was extremely energized. I never felt so alive in my life.

This was the first time in my life that I actually felt like I was worth anything. Tonight some total stranger was going to pay a small fortune for the right to own me. When I was a high priced hustler for my lover's modeling agency, in Los Angeles. I really got off on the fact that I was paid $300 an hour to do what I like to do, please men. But, that was small change compared to the high that I now felt.

As I waited for my number to be called I tried to understand how I had changed so much, or had I? My master had taken me from a submission, shy, young man and transformed me into a very committed man slave.

Was it the physical training, the countless hours of learning to follow my master's orders, or was it the machine that did it? Yes, the machine. Twice a week I was taken to a special room in my master's house and hooked up to a machine. I was given a helmet, with wires attached, to wear. I was then ordered to relax on a small bed and just listen.

The music that was played was mostly nature sounds and it quickly put me to sleep. Each time I woke up I seemed to be more devoted to my life as a slave. Whatever the reason, I am, what I am, a devoted man slave.

Suddenly, the attendant told me to get ready I had 3 minutes to get ready. As I got to my feet, beads of sweat started to run down my naked body, as my cock throbbed so hard that I felt like cumming right then and there. I put on my number chain and started out the door. As I walked down the hallway I could hear music being played. People in the hallway stopped what they were doing and stared at my muscular naked body and big hard cock. They seemed pleased and most of them smiled. As I stood behind the stage curtains some of the backstage crew patted me on my bare ass, tickled my balls and played with my pulsating cock. All of which made me even hornier.

As my number was called I felt a surge of sexual energy flow though my body. I parted the curtains and started to walk down the runway. All the way down the runway my big stiff cock just bounced against my stomach. I got more and more turned on as I realized that several hundred men were visually raping my naked body. The approving sounds from the audience just made me feel more energized. I smiled, as I mounted the auction platform.

As I stood on the posing platform the sounds of the audience died down, the auction was starting. The overhead lights went on and the auctioneer walked up to stand beside me. My master quickly looked over my naked body and smiled. My master looked very pleased. He then started to point out my best points and to describe how will trained I was. He finished his introduction of me by showing off one of my talents, he ordered me to cum without touching myself. I was so turned on that cumming was easy. In less than a minute I shot several streams of warm, sticky cum several feet into the air.

As cum and sweat ran down my naked body my master began the bidding. That night I sold for the highest price of the auction, 1.2 million dollars. It was a figure that shocked the hell out of me, but it made my master proud of me. As the attendant led me away the audience wildly clapped. I smiled. I had pleased my master one more time and I had had the wildest experience of my life, and that was all that mattered to me.

The attendant led me to a small room that was being used as a holding room for sold slaves. The slaves that had been sold before me were sitting on wooden stools with their arms tied behind their backs. One plain mattress covered part of the floor.

The attendant tied my arms behind me and told me to sit on one of the stools and to remain silent. He told me that my new master would claim me as soon as the money transfer took place. I sat down and kept quiet. As I waited for my new master to show up I looked over the other slaves in the room. They were all calm like me except for a young pretty blond boy. He was the same blond boy that I had seen at the pre-show, the one that barely looked 18 years old. His body shook and his eyes had a scared look in them. I was to find out the reasons for his sense of fear later.

I sat silently for almost an hour before an attendant and a new master came to claim his property. An Asian man claimed a good-looking young Hispanic slave and walked out of the room.

The second master to claim a slave was a completely different story. He was a good-looking, longhaired blond man, who was in his 30's. He looked great, but there was something about his eyes and the vibrations that I got from him that told me he was trouble.

My eyes caught his and my body tensed up. Was this man my new master? The man smiled at me and my heart sank. I felt like I was really in trouble until the man broke eye contact with me and looked directly at the young blond pretty boy.

The blond boy moaned really loud and his body started to shake as he said, "Oh no, not you." The young slave seemed to know the man. The longhaired blond master smiled a little before he walked over and claimed the scared, young man as his property. The young man's new master ordered him to stand up and he obeyed. The boy's master than untied the slave and for the next 15 minutes or so, he brutally inspected his new slave's naked body. He pulled on his nipples so hard that he yelled and he squeezed his ball until the boy almost passed out.

After he was though inspecting his new property the blond master grabbed his slave by the shoulders and threw him on to the mattress. The boy's master than took off his robe, exposing a big and hard throbbing cock. This whole brutal scene had really turned on the man. He put some lube on his hard cock and then he bent down and shoved his big cock all the way up his slave's ass. The young slave screamed and his body shook as the slave's new master shoved it to him long and hard. The more that the young slave showed that he was in pain the more his new master shoved it to him. The boy's new master really liked to inflect pain on him he really got off on it.

After the new master had fucked his slave long and hard for almost a half hour he finally shot his load up the slave's ass and he withdrew. But, he was not done. He had a crazy glazed look in his eyes. As the young slave lay motionless on the mattress his master leaned forward and put his hands on the boy's shoulders. Suddenly, the boy's master clawed his way down the boy's back, across his ass and down the back of his legs. The boy screamed and started to cry. The new master had left fingernail marks all the way down his slave's body and some of the marks were so deep that they were bleeding.

The boy was still crying as his new master yanked him to his feet. He was told to put on his robe and sandals and he obeyed. As the new master took his slave away I felt a sign of relief, thank god that brutal bastard was not my master.

The next master to enter the room was a rugged, stern looking man in his early 40's. He looked straight at me and didn't say a word or smile, he just walked over to me and grabbed me by the hair on the back of my head and yanked me to my feet. When I was standing upright he let go of my hair and he looked into my eyes, "Boy I am your new master. I now own you and I expect to get a lot of use out of you. Do you understand Boy?"

Yes Sir, I will serve you well Sir!"

"You had better Boy, you cost me a lot and I intend to get my money worth out of you."

My new master now started to inspect me, he at first just walked around me and then he ran his hands all over my naked body. My big cock remained throbbing hard. This fact was not lost on my new master. He grabbed my hard cock and said, "Good, you are a really horny slave. Boy how many times can you got off in one day?"

"I can cum up to 10 times in one day, if you want me to Sir!"

"Boy how long can you go without cumming?"

"I can go without cumming for months, if that is what you want Sir!"

"Boy how experienced are you at cock sucking and are you a good fuck?"

"I am a very experienced cock sucker and I have been told that I am a really great fuck Sir!"

My new master smiled, he seemed to like my answers. He started to unzip his pants and he pulled out a nice 8-inch cock.

"O.K. experienced cock sucker let's see how good you are. Get on your knees, Boy!"

"Yes Sir."

I had swallowed my master's cock clear down to his hair and began to give him the best blowjob that I had ever given anyone. I started to think of what a lucky slave I was to have been sold to a master with such a nice man sized cock.

After sucking on my new master's beautiful man cock for about 10 minutes, I felt his legs shake and he started to moan. My master let out a load moan and his cock started to swell just before started to shot a big load of man cum down my throat. I licked the last drops of cum off his still hard cock before I was stopped. My master grabbed me by the hair on the back of my head and he pulled me onto my feet. I bowed my head and put my hands behind my back.

"Boy you were not kidding when you said you were a good cock sucker. Now I am going to find out what sort of fuck you are."

My master led me over to the mattress and ordered me to lay face down. I soon felt a greased cock slid up my ass as my body tensed up and I started to moan. After a half hour of good fucking I felt my master shot his load up my ass. I was so turned on I almost lost my load. My master withdrew and he slapped my ass several times. He seemed very pleased with my performance.

"Well Boy, you are one fantastic fuck and I intend to get a lot of good fucking out of you in the next few years. Boy, get up and put on your robe and sandals, we are going to fly to my island."

"Yes Sir!"

As I got dressed I couldn't help but think, God, my new master is a ruggedly handsome man and he has a beautiful man sized cock. He is also, a really good top and he owns his own island. Man, I am one lucky slave.

CHAPTER FIFTEEN

THE DEAL

Would you ever consider letting a man train you to be his slave, even if that man was really hot and it would only be for a year? That is the question that I have to answer in the next few weeks.

Why is a good-looking, young gay man like me seriously considering devoting a year of my life to serving and pleasing just one man when I could have most any man I wanted? Well, it has to do with my lover James.

My lover is a well-educated, wealthy, 29 year old, good-looking, successful businessman. He was born into a very rich Southern California family and like many over educated, born rich guys he is a little jaded and easily bored. That's where I fit into his life.

I am sort of a gay version of a Hollywood wife. I'm what people call "Eye candy." I have no illusions that my relationship with my lover is based on true love. I'm here because nature was good to me and I can give my lover what he wants and for no other reason.

What does my lover want? He really into kinky stuff and since I am an actor I can usually give him what he wants. That was until just a few weeks ago when he sprung this slave thing on me.

It all started when we went out for dinner at an expensive restaurant on Santa Monica Blvd. I knew from the way my lover was acting that he had something on his mind and as usual that something involved me.

We were seated at an isolated table, away from other customers. This was a dead giveaway that my lover had another kinky idea up his sleeve. After we had ordered our meals James looked directly into my eyes and said, "Babe, I need you to be my slave for a three day weekend."

I didn't know what to say at first. "What do you mean James?"

"It's the same type of acting job that you did at the baths in Chicago, during leather week last year."

"You mean I will have to shave my body hair off and wear a hood on my head again?"

"Hell that was one wild night."

"No, this time you can keep your body hair and we will not need the hood."

"This will be something completely new. I have a very rich uncle, who owns a large ranch in Texas and he has asked me to visit him for a few days."

James now looked down at the table, like a little boy who had done something wrong. "You see, I owe my uncle a lot. He has helped me out a great deal with my life and my finances. The man is an investment genius."

James stopped talking for a moment as if he could not find the right words. "Well, to put it simply, my uncle is what you would call a leather master who owns two well-trained, man slaves and

I kind of went overboard and told him that you were my personal slave. He is now very eager to meet you. You are a good actor and I know that you can handle it."

I had to think for a minute before I answered. "Yes, I can handle a scene like this, but it will cost you."

"Would a three week trip to Europe interest you?"

My eyes lit up and I said, "It's a deal, master."

We flew into Austin, Texas during the night. Early the next morning we rented a car and drove for two hours to reach the ranch. As we drove up to the ranch I could see that three men were working in the barn. It was Uncle John and his two man slaves.

After parking in front of the barn my master told me to get out of the car. I was ordered to strip and to stand submissively, as my master went into the barn to talk to his uncle. As I waited for my master to return, the hot, humid morning air caused me to break out in a heavy sweat. As I stood submissively, I watched little beads of sweat form and start to slide down my naked body.

When my master returned he ordered me to follow him. In the barn were three men in overalls, boots and no shirts. I was not introduced to anyone. I was then ordered to stand in a submissive manner as my master started to talk to his uncle. "Uncle John, this is my slave."

"Well, James does he have a name?"

"No Sir, his name used to be Brad, but I changed it to just Slave. "Would you like to inspect my property uncle?"

"Yes, I would. But, since you have never seen my two slaves Jim and Zack, you can inspect them now if you want."

Master John than ordered his two man slaves to strip and stand for inspection. My master looked very pleased at the prospect of inspecting every inch of their naked bodies.

As Master John started his inspection of me I had a great view of his two man slaves. Jim was an average looking young man of about 28 years of age. He was about 6 foot in height and he had a very muscular and extremely well-defined body. What was really striking about him was that the only hair on his body was his eyebrows. He also had about 9 inches of man meat between his legs with a thick, two-inch silver cock ring attached to the end of it.

Physically, Zack was almost the opposite of Jim. He was probably about 5 foot 9 inches in height. He was also very good-looking. He had short red hair, beautiful smooth skin, a little public hair and a very muscular, well-defined body. Looking at the both of them made me feel a little nervous. These two very well-trained and seemingly devoted man slaves were sort of my competition. Next to them could I measure up?

My master had told me very little about what his uncle looked like other than he was 44 years old. I had expected his uncle to be some fat old fart. But, the man inspecting my naked body was, like his two slaves, extremely well-built and he did not look a day over his early 30's. What really turned me on about him was not just his physical appearance, but his manner. He had a very dominate, commanding presence about him. The feel of his strong hands on my naked body soon had my big cock standing at attention.

When Master John and my master were done with their inspections we slaves were ordered to follow them into the main house as our masters continued to talk. As I followed Master John's two naked slaves I was getting really turned on just watching their beautiful, muscular backsides. Man, these guys have great looking bodies.

When we walked into the main house, Master John ordered me to follow him upstairs, while my master was left in the living to be entertained by his two slaves. When we got to what I think was Master John's bedroom, a very large room, with a marble fireplace, a king size bed and a small office, I was ordered to get on my knees. I quickly obeyed.

I soon hear the sound of Master John taking off some of his clothes. Suddenly, a bare footman was standing in front of me. "Slave, sit up and look at me."

"Yes Sir!"

I faced my master. He was wearing only his boxer shorts and he looked at me with a very cold stare. My body tensed up. I did not know what to expect.

"Slave your master has given you to me for the next three days and I expect to find out as much about your abilities as I can. Let's start by finding out how good you are at licking your master's feet."

He now leaned forward, grabbed me by the hair on the back of my head and forced my head down to his right foot. "Lick my foot Slave!"

"Yes Sir."

I quickly started to bathe his foot in warm saliva and after only a few minutes my master moved my head over to his other foot. I was being trained in how to do it right.

After finishing with his feet, my master gave me instruction in how to lick his nipple and armpits. I was getting so turned on by the way this strong man was using me for his pleasure that my cock was wildly throbbing up and down.

After finishing with his pits my master pushed me backward to stand straight on my feet. As he looked directly into my eyes he quickly took off his boxer shorts and said, "Good work Slave. Now get on your knees and lick your master's balls."

"Yes Sir!"

I felt like a hungry dog that was going to be fed. My master pushed my head forward burying my face in his crotch and for the next several minutes he directed me in how to lick his balls. The manly smell of his crotch and the sight of his big cock throbbing just above my head had me so hot that I had to grab my cock by the head and squeeze really hard to stop myself from cumming. Finally, after my master seemed to be satisfied with my performance he pulled my head off of his balls and put his throbbing cock up again my lips.

"O.K. Slave, get it wet."

I licked my way up one side and down the other and then I quickly swallowed as much of his man meat as I could. I than started to slowly tongue my way back up his cock until I was massaging the head of his cock with my tongue. His body started to shake and he moaned a little. He was getting turned-on. Then suddenly, my master shoved his big cock clear down my throat. I gagged.

"Suck it all Slave!"

When my throat had adjusted I started to deep throat his cock, again and again. My master's moans now grew louder and louder and his legs began to really shake, as I sucked faster and faster.

After only about 5 minutes of the best deep throat cock sucking that I had ever given a man, his body began to violently shake. Just as he let out a loud moan and his cock started to stiffen he shoved his big cock down my throat again and shot his load.

When my master's cock was spent his body relaxed. He then slid his cock out of my mouth and I started to lick it clean, until he stopped me.

He was not done with me. My master now ordered me to stand up just before he pushed me backwards on to his bed.

He then grabbed me by my ankles, flipped me over on to my stomach, and spread my legs far apart with his knees, exposing my asshole. I quickly felt several greased fingers slid deep into my asshole and begin to lubricate and massage the inner tissue of my hole. I started to softly moan as I moved my ass up and down, forcing my master's fingers to move deeper into my ass. Suddenly, the fingers were removed and I felt my master's big cock thrust deep into my anus, causing me to grab hold of the mattress as my body began to slide forward. He then proceeded to royally fuck me in every possible position. Each time he found an angle that really turned me on he would really shove it to me, causing me to moan and squirm, until I was almost at the point of climax, than he would grab the head of my throbbing hard cock and squeeze it really hard until my body relaxed. Just like when I was licking his body my master was still testing me.

My master fucked me for almost an hour and he shot his load another two times. But, the whole time he was fucking me he did not let me cum. "Slaves," he said, "serve better if they are kept horny."

We than took a quick shower. Afterward he let me cuddle up naked next to him in bed, with my head on his muscular chest as we both got a few hours of needed sleep.

All the slaves on Master John's ranch had a job and I was no different. I was given the job of being the house slave. I kept care of the house chores, cooked the meals and sexually pleased the master of the house. I did not wear any clothes for the next three days.

On the third and last day of our stay at the ranch, when we were about to leave, my real master James ordered me to not get dressed and to follow him. He led me out to the barn. The feel of the hot, humid Texas weather had me sweating like a pig by the time we entered the barn.

Master John was in the barn alone and ordered me to stand on a bale of hay. He then briefly inspected my naked, sweat-covered body before he started to talk to my master.

"Well James, I'm impressed with your slave so far. He is really great sex and he is fairly well trained. Frankly, I could train him better."

My master smiled a little. "Yes Uncle John, you are the expert. I'm sure that you could do better."

"Yes, I could and that is why I would like to know if you would like to sell your slave to me? I will give you a very good price for him."

My master got a startled look in his eyes, but he did not lose his composure. He just swallowed hard and said, "Well, no uncle, he is too valuable to me. I would never sell him. Slaves like him are just too rare."

I felt very relieved. Master John now turned around and ran his hands over my bare ass and then he briefly grabbed and squeezed my balls really hard. My body tensed up until he released his grip.

"Well James, if I can't buy him maybe you will let me have him for a year for training. I will be training a friend's slave prospect, starting in two months. It would be a pleasure to add your slave to the program.

I will make you an interesting offer that I think will be a basis for a deal. If you let me have your slave for a year of training I will give your slave a trust fund of $200,000, which I will manage for him until he is no longer a slave. This is the same type of deal I gave my own two slaves. The only difference is that they are on 5-year contracts and their trust funds get only $100,000 a year. I will also sweeten the deal. I will give you the use of one of my slaves for a year to tend to your needs as an added bonus. After one year I will return your slave and you will return mine.

When you get your property back he will be very well trained and he will have an extra 20 to 30 pounds of well-defined muscle on his frame. All in all, he will be a more valuable property when I get done with him."

"I know that it is a great deal, but I will have to think it over for a while if I may? I will let you know in about a month." Master John smiled.

On the trip back to the airport my lover did not speak for the first half hour. I know the mood. He was interested in the deal. I know from what I saw at the ranch that he really wanted that cute, red-haired slave. The idea of being a real master, with a very well trained, good-looking slave, for a year was really turning him on. But, my kinky lover had one problem in making the deal, me.

After getting a little tired of the silence I had to ask him. "James, tell me the truth, would you really have sold me if you had actually owned me?" He remained silence for a moment, as if he were trying to think of what to say.

"Well...no of course not. I wouldn't do that to you, even if it is a great opportunity for you to get some financial security in your life."

He was right about the security thing. I had only made $30,000 or so in my three years of acting. I wasn't making a living by being an actor. I was living off of my rich lover, which long term is not a good idea.

"You know Babe you could sell yourself for a year."

He was now smiling. My lover had finally figured out an angle to work.

"Well, I will have to think about it. I will let you know my answer when we get back from Europe."

My lover looked pleased. I was thinking about it. He knew he was half way home.

Am I going to take the offer? You are damn right I am! The idea of being completely owned and intensively trained for a year, by a real dominate, experienced, hot stud makes my blood boil and that's not every considering the trust fund offer. But, for now I am just going to let my lover sweat for a while.

ABOUT THE AUTHOR

Richard Andrews is a lifetime student of Human Behavior and of Economic and Social Trends in American Society. He has written many short stories that have been printed in such magazines as *Honcho, Torso,* and *Mandate*. Mr. Andrews is now a high school teacher who lives in California.

Richard Andrews has written two other books, *The New Order* and *Ransom Slave*.